FREEBOOTY

Freebooty

A Novel
of Suspense
by Jack Foxx

THE BOBBS-MERRILL COMPANY, INC.
Indianapolis / New York

Library of Congress Cataloging in Publication Data
Foxx, Jack.
  Freebooty.

  I. Title.
PZ4.F7958Fr   (PS3556.098)   813'.5'4   76-1985
ISBN 0-672-52213-6

For my mother-in-law
and my father-in-law,
Waltraut and Bruno Schier

"Five cents a glass!" Does anyone think
That this is really the price of a drink?

The price of a drink! Let him decide
Who has lost his courage and lost his pride,
And lies a groveling heap of clay
Not far removed from a beast today.

The price of a drink! Let that one tell
Who sleeps tonight in a murderer's cell,
And feels within him the fires of hell.
Honor and virtue, love and truth,
All the glory and pride of youth,
Hopes of manhood, the wreath of fame,
High endeavor and noble aim,
These are the treasures thrown away,
As the price of a drink, from day to day.

"Five cents a glass!" How Satan laughed
As over the bar the young man quaffed
The beaded liquor, for the demon knew
The terrible work that drink would do;
And before morning the victim lay
With his life-blood ebbing swiftly away.
And that was the price he paid, alas!
For the pleasure of taking a social glass.

—JOSEPHINE POLLARD

Josephine Pollard is a horse's ass.

—FERGUS O'HARA

FREEBOOTY

1

When the carriage drew up on the dusty corner of Montgomery and Sutter streets, and the driver called out, "Lick House, folks!" Fergus and Hattie O'Hara leaned out from opposite seats for their first look at the hotel. It had been recommended to them by a man on the ferry from Marin—an agent for the shipping line—and it seemed to live up to the recommendation as San Francisco's newest and finest luxury lodging house: three-storied, English Roman in design, shining a polished gray-white in the March sunlight.

O'Hara opened the door, stepped down, and then reached back inside for his wife's hand. He smiled cheerfully as she alighted and began to smooth the wrinkles out of her gray serge traveling dress. "Well now, Hattie," he said, "ain't this a fine-looking hostelry?" He spoke mostly with a thick, careless brogue, the result of a strict ethnic upbringing in the tough Irish Channel section of New Orleans. At times this caused certain ignorant and semi-ignorant individuals to underestimate his capabilities and his intelligence; in his profession, this had proved to be a major asset.

Hattie said, "It does seem quite grand."

"As fine as any in Saint Louis or Chicago. San Francisco is a city of consequence, my lady."

"It'll do for a brief visit."

"Only that?"

"I've never been partial to hills, Fergus."

O'Hara laughed. "The hills are part of its charm," he said expansively. "Ah, Hattie, can't you smell the tang of salt in the air! Can't you fair smell the aroma of spices from the mysterious Orient? Can't you smell—"

One of the carriage horses chose that moment to raise its tail and relieve itself, loudly and moistly.

Hattie wrinkled her nose. "You were saying?"

"I was saying," O'Hara said, undaunted, "that you'll enjoy the shopping here. Silks and laces from the great ports of China. Brocades from the distant provinces of India. You'll have most of the day tomorrow to browse among these fineries, and perhaps to be making a purchase or two."

Hattie looked thoughtful.

O'Hara saw that the carriage driver had nearly finished unloading their luggage: two large carpetbags, two hatboxes belonging to Hattie, and his banjo case. He took her arm, and they started toward the Lick House's entrance.

They made a striking pair, mainly because of the contrasts between them. Tiny, slender, and fair—half Irish and half Pennsylvania Dutch—Hattie was in her late twenties, five years younger than O'Hara. Thick light-brown hair, worn in ringlets, was covered by a traveling bonnet decorated with wisps of white lace. O'Hara, on the other hand, was tall and plump; he sported a luxuriant red beard of which he was inordinately proud and on which he doted every morning with scissors and comb. Like Hattie, he had soft blue eyes; unlike Hattie, and as a result of a vast fondness for any type of so-called Demon Rum, he possessed a rather thick and well-veined nose which approximated the color of his beard. He was dressed in a black broadcloth frock coat, vest and trousers to match, and Wellington boots. He carried no visible weapons, but in a specially constructed pocket holster inside his coat was a double-action Navy .36 caliber Starr revolver.

They entered the hotel lobby. It was huge, with marble floors and immense paintings of California mountain scenes. Mahogany woodwork shone like glass. The furniture was velvet plush, the half-dozen chandeliers crystal, and the pillars flanking the entrance to a massive dining room ornately carved Italian marble.

"Quite grand indeed," Hattie said, impressed.

At the desk, O'Hara secured a room for the night from a prim-looking clerk. When he had finished signing the register, he noticed to one side a neat row of the latest editions of local newspapers. Since he had not seen a paper in three days, he picked up one from the nearest stack—a *Daily Alta California*—and scanned the front page. It was devoted entirely to war news from the East, all of it at least ten days old, since it had been brought to San Francisco overland via Pony Express. The most prominent story told of the March 3rd signing by President Lincoln of the first draft law in the nation's history, and of the furor this had caused among Lincoln's opponents in Congress.

According to Major General Joseph Hooker, who was now in command of the Army of the Potomac, the draft was what was needed to help rebuild the army's shattered units after the ordeal at Fredericksburg in December of the previous year, 1862. The prospect for a Union victory looked better at present, Hooker said, than at any time since the beginning of the war—particularly now that there were reports that the South was short of funds and threatened with bankruptcy.

O'Hara tucked the edition into his coat pocket, paid the carriage driver who had come in with their luggage, and then, with Hattie, followed a liveried bell captain up a winding staircase to their two-room suite on the second floor. Spacious and opulent, it contained, among other appointments, a large four-poster bed which O'Hara eyed with some expectation. He and Hattie had been forced to sleep in much less luxurious surroundings the past two weeks, and in beds which were not conducive to comfortable sleep or to any of the other forms of endeavor for which beds were made. Hattie, in fact, had flatly refused any manner of trifling on any of the beds which they had encountered the past ten days in Nevada and Northern California. Until now, O'Hara had been feeling extremely frustrated.

When they were alone he opened his carpetbag and treated himself to a drink of prewar Kentucky whisky. "There is something about arriving in a city of consequence," he said serenely, "that never fails to be giving me a momentous thirst."

"Everything gives you a momentous thirst," Hattie said. "But the day is still young, if I make my meaning clear."

"You do." O'Hara capped the flask and returned it to his bag, with considerable if veiled reluctance. "I imagine you'll be wanting to change your things and such as that. So I believe I'll be locating the steamship offices and buying our tickets for Stockton on the morrow."

"If there are any saloons along the route, see that you pass them by."

"Hattie, have you no faith in my self-control?"

"I seem to recall a few lapses in your self-control that have led to trouble in the past. There's work to be done in Stockton, if I need remind you, and I don't fancy any difficulties before we even get there. Besides, it's only two days till St. Patrick's Day."

"I'm not likely to be forgetting that," O'Hara said, "and you needn't worry." He kissed her, stroked the curve of her hip, and then cocked a questioning eyebrow and nodded suggestively in the direction of the four-poster. "What would you say to a bit of trifling when I return?"

Hattie said, "You're a billygoat, Fergus O'Hara."

"Billygoat—or fine stallion?"

She blushed. "Go on with you, braggart. Don't be long."

Downstairs again, O'Hara approached the desk and asked the prim clerk where he might find the offices of a steamship line that serviced Stockton.

"There are several," the clerk said. "Perhaps you might try the Pettibone Steamer Company. Three blocks north on Montgomery, between Sacramento and Clay."

O'Hara thanked him and started across to the entrance. Just as he reached the doors a fat man with muttonchop whiskers and a broad smile stepped up to him. "Excuse me, sir," he said. "I happened to overhear your question to the clerk, and I happen also to be on my way to the Pettibone Company. Perhaps I might accompany you, show you the way?"

The fat man wore a brown velvet sack coat, light-colored trousers, and a soft felt hat; an expensive Albert watch chain rested on the bulging front of his vest. He was in his fifties, and his eyes were both shrewd and friendly behind ridges of flesh. O'Hara decided he was respectable.

"Permit me to introduce myself," the fat man said. "My name is Horace T. Goatleg."

O'Hara blinked. "Begging your pardon, I thought you said your name was *Goatleg.*"

The fat man made a rumbling noise that O'Hara supposed was a laugh. "I did, sir, I did. Everyone I meet has the same reaction. My parents were German immigrants, you see, and the family name is Ziegenbein. Much too difficult for the average American to pronounce, so my father, after a time, changed it to the literal English equivalent: Goatleg. He had a marvelous sense of humor, my father. I like to think I inherited it."

With a name like Goatleg, O'Hara thought, a man had best have a sense of humor. He introduced himself and said that he wouldn't mind being shown to the Pettibone offices, since he was newly arrived in San Francisco.

"What are your impressions of the city thus far?" Goatleg asked as they went out and turned north along the plank sidewalk.

"A city of consequence," O'Hara said. He liked the phrase.

"Indeed, sir. Indeed. When did you arrive?"

"Only a short while ago this afternoon."

"Well, you must sample our night life. We have theatres to rival any in the East, for example. You've heard of Adah Menken, surely? She is drawing enormous crowds here at the moment in *Wild Horse of Tartary*."

"I've never been much of a one for playacting, Mr. Goatleg, if you'll pardon my saying it."

"Oh, of course, of course." The fat man tugged thoughtfully at one of his chins, looking very much like a spokesman for the Chamber of Commerce. "The Bella Union, then," he said at length. "Also a theatre, sir, but a stag one on the periphery of the Barbary Coast. Not at all like any other theatre you've ever attended." He winked. "The saying hereabouts is that you've not seen San Francisco until you've seen the Bella Union."

"I'll keep that in mind, Mr. Goatleg."

"Good. Excellent. If there is anything I can do, don't hesitate to ask. I've a suite of rooms at the Lick House, you know."

"You must be a successful man to afford such as that."

"Moderately so. I deal in land development—a lucrative profession, with the building boom going on at the present."

"I can see that it would be."

"May I ask what business you're in, sir?"

O'Hara touched his breast pocket automatically; inside was his billfold, and inside that the documents revealing him to be a Pinkerton detective. However, he had no intention of showing these to Goatleg or to anyone else; his reasons for being in California were not for public knowledge. He said, "Well, you might say an arbitrator of disputes is what I am."

"Really? What manner of disputes?"

"My firm in Chicago handles what you could be calling the public relations of certain of the railroads and stage lines. It's my job to settle any difficulties these companies might be having."

"Such as public complaints over services, do you mean?"

"Among other matters."

"You must do a considerable amount of traveling, then."

"My wife and I have covered most states and territories in the West and Midwest."

"Your wife accompanies you in your work?"

"She does. She's an unofficial employee of my firm."

"A woman?" Goatleg said incredulously.

O'Hara bristled a little. "And why not? You can appreciate that a woman's touch is required in certain disputes, can't you?"

"Oh, well, I suppose I can," Goatleg said. The look on his face, however, said that he thought a woman had no place in any type of business activity. "Is it your work that is taking you to Stockton?"

"It is."

"When do you expect to be leaving?"

"On the morrow."

"Ah, then we shall be companions on the *Freebooty*. I'm off to Stockton myself tomorrow, as it happens. Also on business."

"*Freebooty?*" O'Hara said. "That's a curious name for a steamboat."

"Not so curious as my own name, sir, but curious nonetheless, I admit. How the packet came to be called that is an interesting tale. Old Pettibone, you see, owned a great fondness for stud poker, and in a game eight years ago he won her from the proprietor of a rival company—a game which the rival claimed was crooked as a goat's leg." The fat man made the rumbling sound again. "Whether or not it *was* crooked was never proved. Pettibone took over the packet, and not so privately referred to her as his freebooty. Shortly afterward, he changed her name to that from the *Delta Star*. He had a fine sense of humor, by God."

"Had?"

"He was shot dead six months later. Caught cheating at stud poker." Goatleg rumbled once more, as if he thought Pettibone's death was a very good joke. "The old man's sons, who operate the company now, have not seen fit to change the name of the steamer a second time. Something of a monument to the rapacity of their father, I expect."

They had reached the corner of Sacramento and Montgomery. Across the street, workers were constructing a building that would one day be, according to a large sign, the Donahue, Kelly Bank. Landaus and stanhopes and broughams clattered past on the dusty street, along with a Wieland's Brewery wagon and a man riding a high-wheeled "boneshaker" bicycle. Expensively dressed men in top hats entered and came out of brokerage houses, office buildings, banks, and express and steamship company offices.

The more O'Hara saw of San Francisco, the more impressed he was by it. It had undergone a period of depression and upheaval in the fifties, he knew, largely because of the decline in gold yield from the placer mines and of the social problems which had been compounded rather than solved by the two Committees of Vigilance; but the discovery of silver in Nevada had ended that era and brought about a new prosperity and a mushrooming population of nearly sixty thousand. San Francisco capital controlled the greater number of Nevada mines, and local industry furnished not only necessary machinery for mining and reducing ore, but most of the necessities and all of the luxuries for residents of the rich silver towns.

A boy in a slouch cap came toward O'Hara and Goatleg with an armful of the current edition of the *Daily Alta California,* shouting out the war news headlines. The fat man commented, "Tragic business, the war."

"As war always is," O'Hara agreed.

"It does appear as though the tide is beginning to swing in favor of the Union."

"Perhaps. You can never tell what might happen."

Goatleg gave him a sidelong glance. "You *are* pro-Union?"

"My head is. My heart ain't so sure."

"Meaning, sir?"

"Meaning only that I was born in New Orleans and had my growing up along The Levee. I'm a Southerner by birth and sympathy, Mr. Goatleg. But I've spent all my adult years in the North, and supported the politics of Mr. President Lincoln, and I can't say as I'm able to be condoning secession and the attitudes of pro-slavery."

"I can appreciate how you feel," Goatleg said. "I

can, indeed. I was born in Atlanta myself, as it happens."

"Were you now?"

"My family moved West when I was a youngster, but I have never truly forgotten the South. No man who was raised in those gentle states can ever truly forget them, can he? Or expel the pulse of them from his blood?"

O'Hara nodded solemnly.

They had crossed Clay Street, and just ahead was a new brick building with a wooden signboard above the entrance that said PETTIBONE STEAMER COMPANY. Goatleg led the way inside. The offices were large and jammed with a heterogeneous crowd waiting in ragged queues to purchase riverboat passage: men and women of almost every class, race, manner of dress, profession, and—judging from the appearance of two hard-eyed ladies near the front—moral fiber.

Goatleg said, "Ah, there's the captain of the *Freebooty,* and Mr. Woodman, the chief pilot." He pointed to two men engaged in conversation on the far side of the room. The captain was in his mid-fifties, wore a gold-braided uniform, and had neatly barbered gray hair, leathery features and an air of quiet authority. The pilot was dressed in simple though well-made clothing and was perhaps twenty years younger; his most notable features were fierce black eyes and thickly even brows that met to form the likeness of an iron bar in the center of his forehead.

Most river packets, O'Hara knew, operated continuously seven days a week, which meant that the *Freebooty* and her officers ought to be in Stockton today rather than here in San Francisco. He said this to Goatleg, who responded, "Normally that would be the case. But the steamer has been out of service for minor repairs the past week. She commences her schedule again tomorrow."

"It's no wonder, then," O'Hara said, "there's such a conflux on hand."

"Yes. If you'll excuse me a moment, I'll say hello to the captain. He's an acquaintance of long standing."

"I'll hold a place in line."

Goatleg moved across to the two men, and O'Hara stepped up to one of the queues. Directly in front of him was a thin woman with a face like a partially squeezed lemon; ahead of her stood a burly, red-shirted miner on whose shoulder perched a multicolored and impressively large parrot. The parrot faced the rear, and seemed to have taken an interest in the thin woman. It had both its glassy eyes fixed on her balefully.

The woman, after a time, began to fidget under this scrutiny. She hugged her purse against her nearly nonexistent breast and kept looking at the parrot and then looking away again. The bird continued to stare at her in its basilisk way.

At length she muttered abashedly, "Nasty, vulgar creature."

And the parrot said, "Goddamn your heathen eyes."

She stiffened. "Oh!"

"Horse dung," the parrot said.

"Oh!"

"Spread those legs, missie," the parrot said, and began to cackle in an obscene tone, leaning toward her and fluffing its wings.

The woman said "Oh!" a third time and turned and fled.

"I'll be a son of a bitch," the parrot said.

The miner looked back, frowned, and rapped the bird sharply on the beak. It transferred its baleful stare to him, which he returned in kind. The parrot relented and tucked its head under its wing, grumbling to itself.

The line moved ahead in rapid order. When O'Hara was tenth from the ticket window, the parrot withdrew its head and looked at him "Goddamn your heathen eyes," it said tentatively. O'Hara raised his hands, clenched them together, and made a strangling motion; then he clicked his tongue to simulate the snapping of bone. The parrot immediately put its head back under its wing.

Goatleg returned at that point, and presently their turn came up at the window. They purchased Stockton passage, both taking the best accommodations the *Freebooty* had to offer: staterooms in the "texas" on the uppermost, weather deck. O'Hara also took for later perusal a company brochure which the clerk offered him.

When he and the fat man had departed again to the street, Goatleg suggested they go somewhere for a drink. O'Hara was tempted, but he resisted the temptation in deference to Hattie, allowing sadly that he ought to be getting back to the Lick House. Goatleg offered his hand and the hope that they might have the opportunity to talk again, O'Hara politely offered the same, and they went their separate ways.

As he walked down Montgomery, O'Hara found himself considering Goatleg's earlier recommendation of the Bella Union. He had heard of the theatre, which apparently sometimes housed legitimate dramatic productions but which more often presented bawdy stage shows that featured ribald songs and partially un-draped female performers. He had also heard of the infamous Barbary Coast, and the prospect of seeing for himself if it was as wicked as its reputation ap-pealed to his spirit of adventure.

Hattie, of course, would not approve of his ven-turing to either place. Hattie, however, did not have to know about it. After all, a man was entitled to a certain amount of covertly innocent adventure, now wasn't he?

2

As matters developed, O'Hara had no difficulty separating himself from Hattie for the evening. After a six o'clock supper in the Lick House's pillared, vaulted and balconied dining room. Hattie admitted to being tired from the day's traveling and from the richness of the meal; although she didn't say so, she was perhaps also tired from the spirited hour she and O'Hara had spent thrashing about in the four-poster after his return from the steamship office—an hour which she had clearly been coveting as much as he. In any case she professed her intention to retire early with *Elsie Venner,* which was a novel by Oliver Wendell Holmes and the latest of the popular fictions she was fond of reading. (O'Hara, when he read anything at all, preferred the Beadle dime novels which had begun appearing three years earlier.)

He said as they started out into the lobby, "I believe I'll be having a brandy in the Gentlemen's Room, and then a stroll about the area. This is a city that demands exploration, in the night as well as the day."

"Mmm. But mark my words of this afternoon,"

Hattie said, though only as a gentle reminder. "Stay shy of trouble, dear."

"I'll be seeking only sights, not devilment," O'Hara told her piously.

They went upstairs together, with O'Hara staying just long enough in their room to unpack his velvet-collared Chesterfield. When he came down again he entered the Gentlemen's Room—a large, comfortable room tastefully appointed with leather furnishings and dark-stained mahogany woodwork; a liquor buffet stretched along one of the walls, and there were a half-dozen heavy tables covered with green baize along another. The only occupants at the moment were a red-jacketed barman, a white-jacketed waiter, two portly banker types reading newspapers through billows of cigar smoke, and three other men at one of the green baize tables.

Two of the latter group were seated opposite each other and appeared to be playing blackjack. The third man, standing beside the dealer, was Horace T. Goatleg.

O'Hara hesitated, asking himself whether or not he cared for any more of the fat man's company on this day. While he was deciding that he didn't, particularly—Goatleg was a bit too inquisitively loquacious to be desirable as a steady companion—the fat man said something to the other two, took a step away from the table, and saw Fergus across the room. He smiled a broad if preoccupied smile, stopped again, and then made a beckoning gesture, which caused both blackjack players to turn and look at O'Hara, which in turn gave O'Hara no alternative except to approach the table.

Goatleg took his hand and squeezed it like someone testing the freshness of a loaf of bread. "What a pity you didn't stop in sooner, Mr. O'Hara," he said. "I'm just about to leave—an engagement for the Adah Menken play I told you about."

"Aye, a pity," O'Hara said blandly.

"At least allow me to introduce you to my good friends Mr. Colfax and Mr. Tanner," and the fat man proceeded to do just that.

Colfax's full name was John A. Colfax. He was a tall, pale, handsome man dressed in a ruffled white shirt and a Prince Albert. O'Hara knew immediately that he was a gambler, not only because of his dress and because he was dealing the game of blackjack, but because his eyes heralded his profession as plainly as if they were windows inscribed with it—gray windows with shades drawn tightly behind them, so that nothing of what lay within was revealed to the onlooker. In O'Hara's experience most gamblers were slightly above the common footpad in honesty and slightly below the average saloon girl in moral character; but he was inclined to tolerate all men, including gamblers, until circumstances dictated otherwise.

Nothing about the second man, Charles Tanner, offered any indication as to his profession—unless you gave credence to general appearances, in which case he might have been either a nervous mortician or a mild-mannered pirate. He was thin, diffident, long-jawed; he wore a black sack coat and rumpled nankeen trousers that were noticeably out of place in the regal atmosphere of the Lick House. He also wore a black patch over his left eye, the which he stroked self-consciously with the forefinger on one hand. The good right eye blinked steadily, as if it were trying to dislodge a speck of dust or some other foreign matter.

"I must hurry," Goatleg said. "A good and pleasant evening to you, Mr. O'Hara. Gentlemen." He beamed at all of them in general and then hurried away toward the lobby exit.

Both Colfax and Tanner seemed to be regarding O'Hara speculatively. The gambler said, "Perhaps you'd care to join us, Mr. O'Hara?" His voice dripped charm and good fellowship like molasses from the mouth of a jug.

Regretfully O'Hara shook his head. "My luck with the pasteboards is sad indeed," he said. "And with all other games of chance as well. So I'm not a gambling man."

Tanner said, "Whore hound?"

O'Hara stared at him narrowly. "What was that?"

The one-eyed man had his right hand inside his coat pocket; he brought it out holding a small candy sack. "Horehound drops," he said. "I asked if you wanted one."

"Oh," O'Hara said. "No, thanks. I don't use 'em."

"Good for the throat."

"No doubt they are, but my own throat favors a bit of after-dinner brandy just now." He caught the waiter's eye and motioned, and when the man approached he ordered a pony of French brandy. The waiter nodded approvingly and went away again.

O'Hara turned back to the two men at the table. Tanner had fed himself some of the hoarhound drops, and you could hear faintly the sound of his sucking on them; his long, meek face said that the taste was more than a little satisfying. Colfax had produced from somewhere half a dozen or so small bronze war-issue cent pieces—coinage that was not often seen in the West, and mostly valueless here as well—and he shuffled them in an habitual fashion in his left hand. Both men were still looking interestedly at O'Hara.

Colfax said, "Have you and Mr. Goatleg been acquainted long?"

"Only since this afternoon," O'Hara answered.

"Was it business that brought you together?"

"No. We met by chance, as it happened."

"Might I ask where you're from?"

"Chicago, at the present."

"Will you be stopping here long?"

"Just until the morrow."

"Business trip? Or pleasure?"

"Business," O'Hara said. "Public relations for the Adams Express line."

"Given any thought to moving West?" Tanner asked abruptly.

"Well, the missus and I have discussed the matter."

"Plenty of opportunity in California—plenty of land."

"Aye, I've seen that there is."

"Ought to speak with Goatleg about it. He's the man to consider if you've spare funds to invest."

"Real estate speculation is a gamble, to my way of thinking," O'Hara said mildly, "and as I've mentioned I'm not a gambling man."

"Hardly a gamble in California," Tanner said.

"Still and all, there are other forms of investment. Non-gambling ones."

"Such as?"

"The kind that guarantees postwar security."

"D'you mean government bonds, Mr. Tanner?"

Colfax said, "Exactly—government bonds. If you're interested, why don't you discuss the matter with Goatleg? He is something of a financial wizard, you know."

"Perhaps I'll be doing that very thing," O'Hara lied, and cast a look to the buffet for his brandy. To his relief he saw that the waiter was on the way with it.

Tanner popped another hoarhound drop into his mouth, stroked his eyepatch, and kept his good eye focused, now, on the table in front of him; he seemed of a sudden to have withdrawn moodily, for no apparent reason. The war-issue cent pieces rattled and clinked in Colfax's hand, and his smile had a large number of sharp white teeth in it, not unlike a wolf's. They were a mightily odd pair, O'Hara thought, and no gainsaying that; and if you included Goatleg, the sum of them was an even odder threesome. He wondered exactly what they had in common, and concluded without much consideration that he didn't care enough to pursue finding out. In fact, he did not especially care to share their company any longer; it was near time for his investigation of the Barbary Coast and of the rumored "sinful pleasures" of the Bella Union.

When the waiter brought his brandy, O'Hara said, "Well gentlemen, I'll not be keeping you from your game." He raised the snifter slightly in a farewell gesture. "I've enjoyed the meeting of you both."

"A mutual pleasure," Colfax said, and dipped the

upper half of his body forward in a seated bow. Tanner said nothing, did not even move; except for the faint sucking sounds he made, and the fluttering of his good eye, he might have been newly dead.

O'Hara went away to the opposite side of the room, found a chair behind a pillar, and drank his brandy in solitude. Then from the pocket of his coat he produced his favorite briar, a plug of black tobacco and a penknife and began to shave off thin cuttings from the plug into the blackened pipe bowl. When it was full and he had tamped it down and lit it to his satisfaction from a wooden match, he put on his Chesterfield and departed into the lobby.

The desk clerk attempted to look even primmer than usual when O'Hara asked him directions to the Bella Union; nevertheless, his eyes betrayed what was, like as not, a repressed lechery. The theatre, he said, was located on the Washington Street side of Portsmouth Plaza, which could be gotten to by walking north on Kearny, which was the next street to the west of Montgomery. The Barbary Coast itself, he said, should the gentleman be foolish enough to want to venture there, had its black heart on Pacific Avenue between Kearny and the waterfront, Pacific Avenue being two blocks to the north of Washington. O'Hara said he thought he had all that straight in his mind, and the clerk sighed primly but a little wistfully, and Fergus winked at him and went on out to Montgomery Street.

He was somewhat surprised, after the clear skies of the afternoon, to find that a loose blanket of fog had draped the taller buildings and obliterated the moon and the stars. Visibility was still good at street level, however, enhanced by the lighted gaslamps stretching along both sides: up the hill until the mist swallowed them fuzzily near the crest, down the hill to where horse-drawn rail cars cast red and green lampglows on Market Street. Lantern-lit carriages clattered past, and there was a goodly amount of foot traffic.

O'Hara turned up the velvet collar of his Chesterfield—the fog was cold and damp and penetrating—and walked rapidly over to Kearny Street and started uphill toward Washington. Kearny was San Francisco's main shopping street; he passed closed stores and some open ones of every persuasion, as well as restaurants and hotels and gentlemen's saloons. In the distance he could hear the oddly lonely sounds of hand-struck fogbells, which would doubtless be guiding night ferries to their slips. The aromas of salt water, woodsmoke, fresh horse manure and his own pipe smoke were heady in his nostrils.

When he was two blocks from the southern boundary of Portsmouth Plaza, O'Hara began to hear the upraised voices of a large and, if the noise was an accurate indication, not very orderly body of men. He peered through the mist and was able to discern crowd movement ahead, in and about the square. He quickened his pace.

The plaza came into view when he neared Clay Street: sparsely treed, thinly illuminated by gaslight, surrounded by a low iron-picket fence—and at the moment filled with men. Hundreds more overflowed the plank sidewalks outside the fences on Clay, Kearny and Washington streets, impeding carriage traffic. Some of those within the square carried flaming torches that gave a crimson tinge to the drifting tracery of fog; others held aloft banners and placards and signboards, each with lettering O'Hara was unable to read at a distance.

Most of the shouting was being done by those in the plaza—some of it good-natured, some of it angry, some of it derisive. Then, as O'Hara reached the corner, a score or more voices burst into spirited song:

John Brown's body lies a-mouldering in the grave;
John Brown's body lies a-mouldering in the grave;
John Brown's body lies a-mouldering in the grave;
 His soul is marching on!
Glory, halle-hallelujah! Glory, halle-hallelujah!
 Glory, halle-hallelujah!
 His soul is marching on!

The song was familiar—O'Hara had heard it on at least half a dozen occasions in the past year; but he had never heard it sung, as it was being sung now, in a lilting and harmonious Irish brogue.

Intrigued, he hurried across Clay Street to find out just what was going on.

⊷3⊷

What was going on, as nearly as O'Hara could tell
from comments made by the crowd as he pushed
through it, was an impromptu confrontation between
pro-Union and pro-Rebel factions. The Rebels had
gotten there first and had begun staging a small-scale
rally on the Washington Street side of the plaza; then
the Union forces had come upon the scene and taken
over the Clay Street side of the plaza. The path down
the center, the only deserted turf in the entire square,
seemed to have become a kind of Mason-Dixon line;
neither side had invaded the other's territory, at least
not yet.

The twenty or more voices were still singing stan-
zas from "John Brown's Body," and O'Hara located
them as soon as he edged in close enough to the fence
for a clear view. There were about thirty of them altogether, grouped to one side of three wooden packing
cases that had been joined to create a platform; all
were wearing blue Union Army forage caps except for
one, who had on a Kossuth hat. Fluttering above them
on a short pole held by one of the group was a green

banner on which were crudely printed in white the words MULROONEY GUARDS, SAN FRANCISCO COMPANY A. Which told O'Hara that they were an Irish company of militiamen: either an official adjunct of the United States Army or an organized civilian outfit.

When the Mulrooneys began the verse, "They will hang Jeff Davis to a sour apple tree!" a roar went up from the Union supporters, and several of their number waved the placards and signboards O'Hara had been unable to read from a distance. Now he could read them easily enough, and there was a disparate array of messages. One of the largest said:

THE UNION THE WHOLE UNION
& NOTHING BUT THE UNION
—Webster

and there were similar quotations from Abraham Lincoln and others. Just inside the fence nearby, a man with a briarlike tangle of whiskers carried a sign that proclaimed dubious sympathies:

FREEDOM FOR ALL MEN AND NEGROS

Still another message, obviously composed by a man who took matters less seriously than most, read:

PISS WHEN YOU CAN, MEN
—U.S. Grant

O'Hara thought this last to be clever but of doubtful authenticity as attributed, since a similar comment had supposedly been made by the Duke of Wellington when asked by a subaltern to contribute a bit of military wisdom.

Across the square some of the Rebels had commenced singing "Dixie"; but there was no group of men alive, as O'Hara well knew, who could out-vocalize thirty harmonizing Irishmen. The Mulrooney Guards raised their voices in the final stanza of "John Brown's Body," and as a result Daniel Emmett's Southern call-to-arms was thoroughly and summarily drowned.

> *Now, three rousing cheers for the Union!*
> *Now, three rousing cheers for the Union!*
> *Now, three rousing cheers for the Union!*
> *As we are marching on!*
> *Glory, halle–hallelujah! Glory, halle–hallelujah!*
> *Glory, halle–hallelujah!*
> *Hip, hip, hip, hip, hurrah!*

The Union supporters cheered lustily, torches and signboards dancing in the air above them. The Southern contingent ceased singing "Dixie" and did some cheering of their own; then one of them stood on a crate and commenced a full-voiced tirade against "the Abolitionist forces of that tyrant Abraham Lincoln, with their war-cry of 'Beauty and Booty' that would cleave out the very heart of the South." Immediately, a Unionist climbed onto the packing-case platform next to the Mulrooney Guards to denounce Confederate General Beauregard, who had coined the "Beauty and Booty" phrase in a proclamation in 1861, as "a murderer, a fool and a traitor." The Rebel shouted that the Union forces were guilty of "unspeakable atrocities" on the battlefield; the Unionist shouted that the Confederate forces were guilty of "heinous acts of barbarism" on the battlefield. The Southerner screamed that Confederate officers were being "tortured like prisoners of the Spanish Inquisition in such black holes as Plattsburgh"; the Northerner bellowed that Libby Prison in Richmond was "known as The Devil's Warehouse because only the descendants of Satan himself could treat human beings so foully."

Both sides were working themselves up to a fever pitch, and it was obvious to O'Hara that a physical confrontation was imminent. The wise thing for him to do, he thought, was to move on elsewhere, lest he find himself caught up accidentally in the spirit of matters. Still, he was reluctant to leave with the outcome of events in doubt, particularly since there were some thirty good Irish lads in the middle of the about-to-be fracas. He decided that a compromise was in order: he would retreat to the rear of the spectator lines and drift along them until the battle commenced, which maneuver would take him out of the danger zone and yet allow him to view the action.

O'Hara smiled to himself, thinking that Hattie would be proud of such foresight and restraint, and turned quickly to start back through the crowd. As he did so, he caught a fleeting glimpse of a familiar face not ten feet away—fleeting because the face ducked down instantly into the collar of a black sack coat, and then a pair of long legs carried it away to the west at a hurried pace.

Charles Tanner, of the eyepatch and hoarhound drops.

Frowning, O'Hara pushed his way out into the middle of Clay Street and started in the wake of the one-eyed man. But it was a futile effort; Tanner was swallowed immediately by the foggy darkness and the milling crush of onlookers.

O'Hara stopped and gnawed reflectively on the stem of his pipe. Had Tanner followed him from the

Lick House? Well, the only conceivable reason for such an action was thievery, and whatever else Tanner had appeared to be, a common footpad was not among the possibilities. Still, it was strange that he should have left the hotel not long after Fergus himself had departed, and then have turned up here at Portsmouth Plaza. And strange, too, that he had taken his leave so abruptly just now—as if O'Hara's sudden turning had caught him unprepared, and he had hastened away rather than stand for another meeting.

Irritation deepened O'Hara's frown into a scowl. He was not fond of mysteries, even such a minor one as this. Since there was nothing to be done about it at the moment, he conveniently forgot about the compromise he had made with himself and took his irascibility back through the crowd—eliciting glares from those he jostled, which he returned in kind—and pushed in close again to the iron-picket fence.

The two rival orators were hurling rhetoric directly at each other now, and their accusations had become even more vitriolic. There were ominous grumblings among the Mulrooney Guards, as well as the other Union supporters; the smaller band of Southerners appeared to be massing together, as though to withstand an assault, or perhaps to perpetrate one of their own. It would not be long, O'Hara thought with tart relish, before the plaza became a minor battleground.

He was right. Less than thirty seconds had passed when the Rebel spokesman called for "the hanging of Abraham Lincoln, a slave-loving, highbinding Judas," and one of the Mulrooney Guards immediately shouted in response, "Begob, no damned Copperhead can talk that way about our President! Agitators, that's what the lot of 'em are! Sons of Liberty—or worse yet, Knights of the Golden Circle!''

Sons of Liberty was a nationwide secret society of Southern secessionist sympathizers living in the North, and the Knights of the Golden Circle was an even more militant offshoot of the group which, it was rumored, was plotting to take control of California and swing its support to the Confederacy. The mere mention of these two hated groups was sufficient to galvanize the Unionists into combat. The Mulrooney Guard wearing the Kossuth hat yelled, ''Sons of Liberty, hell! Sons of *bitches!*'' There was an angry roar of agreement, and the Unionists plunged forward. The Rebels did not wait for the attack; they rushed forward themselves, and the two sides met in the center of the square with a great deal of shouting, clashing bodies, flailing signboards, and swirling torches.

It was apparent to O'Hara that the Union supporters, owing to greater numbers and to the fighting thirty of the Mulrooney Guards, were destined to have the best of the skirmish. But it was also apparent that the Confederates would not be easily routed: they were giving considerable of what they were receiving. One man—it was difficult to tell to what side he belonged—went down, and then a second and a third, the last streaming blood from a gash on the head. A firebrand, dislodged from someone's hand, looped through the air like a firewheel at an Independence Day carnival and landed near the crate on which the Southern orator had been standing earlier; tongues of flame reached out, licked at the crate, and set it to burning—turned it into a leaping pyre whose glare outlined the straining faces of the men fighting nearby.

At almost this same instant, surprisingly enough, O'Hara heard the sudden clamoring of a firebell from the north side of the plaza. A moment later a second firebell sounded to the south. Then two bright red horse-drawn sidestroke fire engines alight with lanterns came charging into view on Kearny Street from opposite directions; simultaneously, a half-dozen helmeted and uniformed policemen emerged from a large stone building across Kearny from the square. The fire engines stopped in the center of the block, the clanging bells ceasing with them. Several firemen—wearing red shirts and high red hats with huge shields affixed to the fronts, on which the numbers of their respective volunteer companies were emblazoned—leaped down and began unraveling hoses and manning hand pumps. The contingent of police stood nearby, managing to look alert and purposeful without doing anything at all.

All of this unexpected and puzzling activity brought a near halt to the fighting in the plaza; except for two or three isolated instances in which oblivious opponents continued to batter each other, Unionists and Rebels alike stood shoulder to shoulder as they watched the firemen and the police. The spectators as well had reversed their attention from plaza to street.

No one, O'Hara included, seemed to know quite what was going on. There was no sign of a fire anywhere except for the burning crate toward the Washington Street end of the plaza, and there was no danger of the crate's setting off a conflagration in any of the buildings neighboring the square. But the firemen continued in a flurry of movement, playing out hoses now across Kearny and between the stone building and the one adjacent to the south, where doubtless there was a cistern.

Then one of the firemen came running out from between the two buildings and gave a signal to the men working the hand pumps on the two engines. Immediately the rest of the firemen lifted the hoses.

When the first spray of water shot out of the nozzles, the red-shirted volunteers stepped forward smartly—and directed the streams in a wide radius at Rebels, Unionists and onlookers alike.

The crowd splintered instantly into astonished fragments that fled in all directions. Torches fell to the grass, to the cinder paths, and were doused. The Mulrooney Guards ran as a body, their green banner flying wetly above them, shouting both Gaelic and American imprecations over their shoulders. The Southern orator tripped and fell and was rolled over half a dozen times by the force of one jet of water before he finally managed to regain his feet and leap the fence on Washington. Others suffered similar fates and indignities.

The firemen, flanked by the policemen, continued into the square itself until they were the only individuals present and the surrounding streets were mostly cleared. Then they shut off the water, retreated to Kearny, folded up their hoses, packed up their machines and departed to their respective engine houses. The policemen remained for a few seconds to satisfy themselves that everything was peaceful and was likely to remain so; then they disappeared inside the stone building on Kearny.

O'Hara had never before seen this particular method of dispersing a large and unruly crowd, but he had to admit that it was most effective. He made the admission, as well as his final observation of events, from the refuge he had been forced to take in an alleyway across Clay Street midway in the block. Like everyone else he had run when the firemen turned the hoses on them, and by using speed and certain hand-and-elbow tactics he had fortunately managed to escape an unwanted and unnecessary bath. His pride was ruffled, although he further admitted—grudgingly—that the authorities could not be blamed for any personal water damage that might have been incurred, since they had acted in the best interests of the citizenry-at-large.

O'Hara straightened his vest and frock coat, re-buttoned his Chesterfield, ran a smoothing hand over his beard, and stepped out again into the misty street. Other people were also beginning to filter quietly back into the area. Under one of the gaslights, he checked his pocket watch and saw that it was now well past nine o'clock. He hurried over to Kearny Street.

When he passed the large stone building, he saw the words CITY HALL etched above the entrance, which explained the policemen who had come from and then returned inside. He also took note of the fact, wryly, that the building adjacent to the City Hall on the north was a large and rather ostentatious gambling house called El Dorado.

As soon as O'Hara reached Washington Street, his attention was drawn immediately to the Bella Union—a two-storied building with red "decoy lamps" illuminating large posters that advertised the theatre's shows. A small mixed group of roughly dressed seamen and handsomely outfitted sharpers and business types had gathered before the box office, and others began appearing from the direction of Pacific Avenue. Joining them, O'Hara listened to a variety of bawdy talk, most of it drunken, and was eventually able to pay fifty cents for admission.

The interior of the Bella Union was smoky and noisy but nicely set up: a circle of curtained boxes more like pigeonholes than anything else, and a wide stage over which at the moment hung a gaudily painted drop curtain. On the curtain was a sign announcing that the next show would begin shortly. There were no pretty waitresses such as—it was rumored—could be found in various stages of undress in certain Barbary Coast haunts, but now and then girls could be seen in the boxes, on one occasion just before the covering curtains were abruptly drawn; probably these were female performers in the show whose further job it would be to sell drinks by whatever persuasion might be necessary.

While O'Hara was looking about for an empty cubicle, he noticed three men in a box near the front. One was the man whom Goatleg had pointed out that afternoon at the Pettibone Steamer Company as Mr. Woodman, the chief pilot of the Stockton riverboat *Freebooty*. The other two were strangers: a tall, slim individual with bushy black hair and a thick mustache, and a young blond man with a round, hairless face. All three of them appeared to have been partaking liberally of Demon Rum, most noticeably Mr. Woodman. O'Hara hoped, considering the perils of river navigation, that the pilot had learned to confine his drinking to off-duty hours and that he was able to function effectively with a hangover. Though he supposed

Woodman had and could: the river pilots of his experience were a toughened bunch, an elite bunch who commanded the highest pay of any steamship officer, and no weak man lasted long in their fraternity.

O'Hara found the bar before he located a place to watch the show, which suited him. He paid the outlandish sum of twenty-five cents for a pony of rye, peered into the indecently low-cut bodice of one of the girls' dresses and decided with virtuous loyalty that Hattie's bosom was much superior, and finally resumed his search for a seat. All of the boxes were occupied, but other late arrivals had begun doubling up; O'Hara did the same, entering the first cubicle he came to that had room enough to hold him, where he found he had joined a balding fat man who kept licking his lips in a hungrily expectant manner; a seaman who smelled rather paradoxically of horse manure; and a swaying little merchant-type who looked and sounded as if he were about to be sick. O'Hara kept a wary eye on this last individual, since he was forced to sit next to him.

The show began at length with several ribald songs, each one sung by a different girl. A great deal of laughter and applause followed; the balding fat man whistled and the seaman leered and the little merchant belched. Then there were two mildly amusing skits, a comedian who told a story about an itinerant drummer and the daughter of a rural landowner which O'Hara thought was hilarious and which he filed away for future reference, and finally another series of songs sung by the procession of female performers, most of whom exhibited more this time of what the seaman referred to in toto and rather poetically as "a dream cargo of milkers and shanks."

When the curtain came down, the audience roared and stamped its feet and demanded more. O'Hara got up quickly and departed the box, not because he had been disappointed in the show—it had delivered enough of its advertised bawdiness to satisfy the imp in him—but because the little merchant's face had taken on a greenish hue and his eyes rolled in their sockets like marbles in milk. The fat man and the seaman followed Fergus—just in time, judging from the sounds that came from the cubicle as he moved for the exit.

Outside, O'Hara started up Kearny toward Pacific Avenue. The fog had gotten thicker and less penetrable; the shimmery lights of a carriage at the Clay and Kearny intersection were barely visible, and the fogbells rang steadily along the rim of the bay. There were far fewer pedestrians abroad than earlier.

The heart of the Barbary Coast turned out to be something of a disappointment. O'Hara had expected, after all the elaborate rumors, an exotic street full of wicked adventure. The wickedness was there, to be sure, but it was tawdry and garish, the whole as familiar and unappealing to him as Adele Street in the Irish Channel in New Orleans. There were Cheap John clothing stores and dancehalls and melodeons and deadfalls and concert saloons and expensive gambling houses; there were prostitutes and bunco steerers and crimps and gamblers and cutthroats; there was laughter and shouting and the tinny beat of pianos and the twang of fiddles and banjos. O'Hara stopped into one of the gambling places: fresco and gilt, large paintings of voluptuous nudes, ceiling-high mirrors, dazzling lights; lady dealers behind long rows of mahogany tables covered in leather, on which were spread gold and silver specie, nuggets, and bags of dust, and over which stood merchants and sailors and miners and professional men and every ethnic group including Chinese and Negro.

O'Hara left almost immediately without buying a drink for himself. He had seen enough of the famed Barbary Coast and had had enough "adventure" for the night as well. He would have a nightcap in the Gentlemen's Room at the Lick House, if the buffet was still open. Or a nightcap from his private bottle, if Hattie proved to be asleep. Or, perhaps and best of all, both.

He walked down Montgomery, toward the three-street intersection with Washington and Columbus Avenue. Unlike on Pacific, the sidewalks here were deserted: it was late now, after midnight, and the cold wet fog eddied as thick as cotton bunting, distorting the light cast by the gaslamps, making it impossible to see more than ten rods ahead. Fogbells continued to ring along the nearby waterfront, and from out on the bay a ship's horn sounded. A horsecar, hidden in the mist, rattled and clanged by in close proximity.

The rhythmic slap of his boot soles on the plank sidewalk echoed hollowly as he neared the center of the block. The mouth of a narrow alley appeared there—and no sooner did he draw abreast of it than a man's frightened voice cried suddenly from within the black confines, "Help, out there! Help!"

Another voice said, "Shut up, damn you!" in muffled tones.

O'Hara stopped. The call for help had been directed to him: the echo of his steps had signaled passage. Automatically he slid his right hand inside his

Chesterfield, inside his frock coat, and grasped the butt of the Navy .36 revolver.

"Please!" the frightened voice shrieked. "He wants to kill me! He—"

The flat crack of a gunshot turned the rest of the sentence into an agonized moan.

O'Hara drew the Navy, acting on impulse and reflex, and ran into the alley. It was like running into a vat of India ink; wet blackness closed around him, and he could see nothing but vague shapes and tendrils of fog that parted just in front of his eyes. Another moan came from not far ahead, softer this time and blurred with pain; there were no other sounds. He put his back against the wall of the building on his right and drew a wooden match out of the Chesterfield's left pocket. Held it up, thumbnail poised on the sulfur head—

And something swung out of the darkness, hit him squarely across the left temple and knocked him over like a ninepin.

4

It was not the first time O'Hara had been hit on or about the head with something—the instrument in this case having been a gun with a hand attached, or so he had dimly perceived in the instant before it struck him—and his skull had withstood harder blows without appreciable damage or loss of consciousness. He did not lose consciousness now, although his thoughts rattled around like pebbles in a tin can. He rolled over onto knees and forearms on the alley floor, which seemed to have been constructed mostly of wooden boxes of Virginia tobacco, and then hoisted himself staggering to his feet. His head throbbed thunderously, and there was a ringing in his ears. He realized he still held both his revolver and the wooden match, and in dazed reflex he leveled the weapon and struck the match with his thumbnail. Light flared, and the alley grew day-bright for a second, enabling him to see the huddled figure of a man lying motionless against the building on the left.

The match flare also let the assailant see O'Hara: the bullet from thirty feet up-alley came within an inch of branding Fergus's right cheek.

O'Hara shook out the match, threw himself to one side, and fired at the muzzle flash. His aim was off; a moment later, the sound of running steps penetrated the ringing in his ears. But his Irish blood had been set to boiling: no damned murdering skalpeen was about to get away free with hitting Fergus O'Hara on the head *and* nearly shooting him. He unleashed a leonine bellow that was loud enough to have rattled window glass and took out blindly after the retreating footfalls.

The alley had seemed uncluttered in the match flare, but the heavy swirls of mist and his own somewhat befogged senses made that perception untrustworthy. So, shaking his head to clear it, he ran with his left hand probing the darkness in front of him. Blood trickled warm and sticky down over his left temple and under his right ear, which only served to add fuel to his already well kindled rage.

The fleeing steps veered off suddenly to the right, vanished momentarily and were replaced by indefinable scraping sounds, and then returned again. O'Hara's mental processes steadied and began working again at optimum capability; he realized there must be a second, north-south alley intersecting this one. He slowed his run, saw the intersection materialize through the fog, and swung himself around the corner into the new passage.

Where, after six paces, he ran directly into a wooden fence.

Down he went on his backside, with a jammed left forefinger and a soon-to-be-bump on his forehead. Cursing inventively, he picked himself up, caught the top of the fence, and scaled its six-foot height. When he dropped down on the other side, he could barely hear the assailant's steps; but the fog was patchier here, and he was able to see all the way to the dull glow of a gaslamp on the street beyond. The alley was empty that far—although he thought he glimpsed a shadow disappearing into the mist on the outer street—and once more he launched himself into pursuit.

Just as he reached the street, a muted thudding noise came from off to the right, followed by a loud, indignant and inebriated cry. O'Hara ran that way, crossing the deserted roadway at a long diagonal. The mist shredded to allow him to see a small man wearing a bowler hat knocked askew, sitting on the sidewalk and shaking his fist in the direction of Montgomery Street.

The small man shouted in a tolerably soused voice, "Hoodlum! Ranger! Sydney Duck! Ought to be strung up!" Then he stopped shouting and stopped shaking his fist; instead, as O'Hara ran past him, he rolled over on his side and immediately began to make snoring sounds.

When O'Hara came to the corner he skidded to a halt, breathing in thick wheezes, and listened. The footsteps, still faint, came now from downhill. Peering intently into the fog, he could just make out the indistinct figure of a running man midway along the block. He resumed the chase.

Visibility was just good enough to enable him to run at maximum speed and to keep the shadowy figure in sight. When it crossed Clay, the next street down, O'Hara was fifteen rods behind. Gaining on him, he thought; it won't be long now, laddybuck. He dashed across Clay. But as he came up onto the sidewalk on the opposite side, the figure ahead abruptly disappeared.

O'Hara's stride faltered, but only for an instant. Another alleyway, he told himself. This proved to be an accurate supposition: he reached the mouth of the passage moments later.

He turned into it: heavy darkness again, and floating dense pockets of mist. He ran along the earthen floor with his left hand out in front of him, as he had done in the other alley, and came to yet another intersection; he slowed just long enough to determine that the footsteps were now coming from the right. He went that way, mindful of such obstructions as wooden fences; but he encountered none here.

The footsteps ceased. Close by, there was the frightened neighing of one horse and then a similar sound from a second.

Breathing thickly through his mouth, O'Hara pulled himself up. The faint glow of a lantern penetrated the fog directly ahead, not more than thirty paces distant; more light, this a pale slender wedge, came from the right. One of the horses whinnied again, and harness leather creaked. He heard nothing else.

He continued forward quickly and cautiously until he could make out the sources of the light. One was a lantern mounted on a wagon drawn by two dray horses which filled the width of the alley, and the other was a partially open door to the right-hand building—an impressive five-story brick structure with grillwork balconies at the second level. Above the door was a sign he could barely read: WHAT CHEER HOUSE.

The wagon was laden with medium-sized kegs or barrels, which indicated a late and probably urgent delivery of some type or other to the hotel. There was no sign at the moment, however, of anyone human. O'Hara drew closer, looking to the right because that direction seemed to offer the largest amount of space for passage around the wagon.

The hurtled object came from the left—one of the kegs or barrels.

O'Hara saw it just in time to pitch his body forward and in toward the hotel wall; it sailed past his head, missing him by very little, and slammed into the bricks. Now kegs and barrels were sturdily built, but even so, if one struck a brick wall at the proper angle and with sufficient force, it had been known to break apart. This one struck the brick wall of the What Cheer House at the proper angle and with sufficient force and promptly broke apart—just as O'Hara rolled over onto his buttocks and put his arm up instinctively to protect his face. Staves and metal strapping and the contents of the keg rained down on him.

The contents, unfortunately, happened to be beer.

The foamy brew got into his eyes and mouth and nose and drenched him from head to foot in sticky, pungent suds. Spluttering, he sat up and shook his head like a bewildered bull—and a gun crashed from behind the wagon. The horses whinnied in terror and reared up, kicking wildly. The bullet made a chinking sound in the bricks two inches from O'Hara's left ear. O'Hara roared forth with a smoky nine-jointed oath, fired blindly in the general direction of the other shot, and scrambled backward through lager mud and foam to escape the plunging hooves of the dray horses. There were shouts from inside the What Cheer House, and then, discernible among them, the resumed pounding of escaping footfalls.

O'Hara lumbered to his feet just as the hotel door opened wide, sending out a brighter and wider swath of light, along with the heads of two curious but circumspect men. Fergus brandished the gun at them, still cursing, and both heads disappeared as if they had never been there at all; the door slammed shut. Then he slid along the wall, rubbing at his beer-stung eyes so that he could determine what the dray horses were doing. When he could see clearly he found that they were still shuffling around in harness, though neither of them was plunging any longer. He pushed past them and the wagon without bodily damage and ran out to Sacramento Street, looking both ways. When he heard the dim sound of steps to his left, he charged off in that direction, dripping lager and foam and thinking only of the pleasantly horrible things he would do to his attacker once he caught him.

The chase from this point covered better than two blocks—O'Hara could hear the running steps a short distance ahead of him all the while—and took them into a warehouse district: the waterfront. Most of the tumble-down buildings were built precariously on mudflats; all of them looked abandoned, although it was unlikely that they were. There were no streetlamps in the area, and the fog was as thick as a Creole gumbo: nothing penetrated it except the odors of salt water and rotting fish and the ever-present clanging of the fogbells.

O'Hara turned a corner after the treads and found himself on a rickety plankway built on pilings which skirted the fronts of at least two of the warehouses. Black, fog-crusted water stretched away on his right. He listened for the steps, heard them running away at an angle to the left. He ran until he came upon a fork in the plankway, took the left artery between two warehouses, saw that that one also forked between these buildings and a new set behind, and was trying to determine which of the paths to follow when a voice said, "Hold on there, matey. What's your hurry?"

O'Hara stopped, peering into the mist for the owner of the voice. He held his revolver down and in against his right hip, concealing it there. Obligingly enough, a man appeared from along the side of a shed-like appendage on one of the warehouses and hurried over to him. The man was dressed in heavy dark clothing, with a dark sailor's cap pulled down low over his eyes; his face shone whitely in the darkness. Despite the gun this newcomer also happened to be holding, O'Hara knew that this was not the man he had been pursuing—knew it because he could still hear the running bootfalls, very faint now and growing fainter by the second.

He looked at the man, looked at the gun, looked in the general direction of his quarry. He said breathlessly, "Did you see which way that blackguard went?"

"Never mind him, matey. You've got plenty enough business with me."

O'Hara shifted his weight impatiently. "What is it you want?"

"Your money and valuables—quick now."

"So you're a bloody footpad, are you?"

"Here, you're in no position to be calling names," the footpad said. He sniffed O'Hara contemptuously. "If you give me trouble, matey, I'll shoot you or knock you on the head and sell your drunken carcass to one of the Shanghai crimps."

"Oh, you will, will you?" O'Hara said, and kicked him squarely between the legs.

The footpad stood straight up, and his face became even whiter under the sailor's cap. He said, "Ung." He dropped the gun and reached for himself with both hands and said, "Rrahh." He fell to his knees and said, "Aaggg."

"Now I asked you a question," O'Hara said. "Which way did that other skalpeen go?"

"Ooog," the footpad said.

"Bah," O'Hara said disgustedly. "Well, I don't suppose it matters much at the present; he's long gone."

"Unnhh," the footpad said.

"It's your own damned fault, lad," O'Hara told him, and hit him on the head with the barrel of his Navy .36. The footpad fell over on his back and did not say anything else.

When he took the left fork in the plankway, O'Hara found himself in a cul-de-sac. He came back and went to the right, and this artery looped around and joined a wheel-rutted street. There was no indication anywhere of the assailant.

In the next block O'Hara located a streetlamp and paused under it to take inventory of himself. His Chesterfield was streaked wetly with grime, and there was a jagged tear at the knee of his trousers; he had a knot on his forehead where he had struck the fence, and the wound on his left temple, though it had stopped bleeding, felt mushy and painful to the touch; his breath wheezed in his throat like an ancient and laboring steam locomotive; and he smelled as though he had bathed in a brewery vat. Nevertheless, he decided—

ruefully—that he had not suffered any serious damage. His only regret was that his assailant had also not suffered any serious damage, or for that matter any damage at all.

He further decided, for two reasons, that what he would do now was to return to the alley where the chase had begun. One reason was that the victim of the initial shooting might still be alive and undiscovered and thus in need of medical aid; the other reason was that the victim, if alive, might possibly be able to tell him the name of the assailant—or that the attacker might have inadvertently left on the premises some clue to his identity. O'Hara had never allowed a personal assault to go unreprisaled, and if it could be helped he did not intend to allow the establishment of a bitter precedent tonight.

Grumbling irritably to himself, trailing beer fumes, he made his way back through the fog to Montgomery Street and up to the alley between Washington and Jackson. Without incident, surprisingly enough.

⊶5⊷

The victim of the shooting was still there, alone in the fog, huddled on the wood-and-earth floor. In the light of a match, O'Hara saw that he was young, not more than twenty-five, and well-dressed. His eyes were squeezed shut, and he had both hands pressed to his stomach and his knees drawn up. Blood stained his fingers and clothing, a great blotch of it. When O'Hara knelt beside him and put a hand inside the frock coat, he felt a faint and irregular heartbeat.

The match burned out and he lit another. This time he started slightly in the flare of light, for the young man's eyes had opened and were staring up at him, glazed with pain. The mouth opened too and the throat worked spasmodically but nothing came out except a thin ribbon of blood.

"Easy, lad," O'Hara said gently. "Easy now."

The young man's mouth continued to work. He managed to make an unintelligible sound, then liquid words that O'Hara could barely hear: "Help . . . me. . . ." Fergus winced: the lad was beyond help and had been from the moment the bullet penetrated his body in the lower stomach; that manner of wound was invariably fatal. "Hurts . . . badly shot . . ." He coughed blood, stopped abruptly and gave a thin sigh.

The second match went out then—and the young man's life with it.

There was a billfold inside the frock coat, and O'Hara withdrew it and flipped it open. By the light of a third match he found identification which stated that the young man had been Thomas A. Stuart, a resident of Mission Street. The billfold also contained forty dollars in greenbacks and four gold double-eagles, a considerable sum of money to have been carrying in or about the Barbary Coast; several cards, a somewhat rumpled playbill advertising the appearance of Adah Menken as Mazeppa in *Wild Horse of Tartary,* and a letter from a cousin in Los Angeles.

O'Hara closed the billfold and put it back inside the dead Mr. Stuart's coat. Then he stood and searched the immediate area as best he could by matchlight. He found nothing that might have been dropped by the assailant or might otherwise point to his identity. Which left not a thing more to be done here. As much as the prospect galled him, it appeared that the attacks on him would have to go unrequited.

He had taken three steps toward Montgomery Street when light cut suddenly through the mist beyond, sought him out. The thud of approaching steps, at least two sets of them, entered the alley at the same time. A young and nervous voice said, "Stand fast, mister. I'm a policeman and well armed."

O'Hara groaned inwardly, but he stood still and waited while the light, which originated from a bull's-eye lantern, bobbed to within two feet of him.

Behind its glare he could just make out the tall form of a helmeted policeman holding an unsteady pistol in his other hand; a second individual, this one helmetless and apparently a civilian, peered even more nervously over his shoulder.

The light wobbled over O'Hara and then slid slightly to the right and behind him, where it picked up and trembled on the body of Thomas Stuart. When it returned finally to O'Hara's face, the young policeman said, "So you've done—" His voice cracked and he had to start over. "So you've done murder tonight, have you?"

If I'd caught that blackguard, O'Hara thought sourly, I might have done murder at that. But he said, "It wasn't me who did for that poor lad."

"No? Then what are you doing here?"

O'Hara explained quickly what had happened.

The policeman seemed partly relieved that he might not, after all, be confronting a murderer, and partly disappointed for the same reason. "You smell as though you've drunk half a keg of beer and poured the other half over yourself," he said suspiciously.

Reminding himself that patience was a virtue, O'Hara elaborated on the beer-keg incident.

"Could he be telling the truth, as far as you know?" the policeman asked the other man.

"Well, I didn't see him on the street, but it was so foggy that I wasn't able to see much of anything. All I know for certain is that I heard a gunshot and came in here and found that man lying over there. That was when I ran around to Kearny Street to summon help and bumped into you."

The policeman scratched his nose indecisively

with the muzzle of his gun, seemed to realize what he was staring into, and snapped the gun down again. The suddenness of that move almost caused him to drop the bull's-eye lantern. He recovered finally and demanded of O'Hara, "Is the victim still alive?"

"No. I've just examined him. I've also just examined his billfold: his name is Thomas A. Stuart. The billfold contains forty dollars in greenbacks and four double-eagles, and you'll be finding it where I returned it inside his coat."

"Mmm," the policeman said. He still sounded indecisive, but he was weakening in the proper direction. "You seem a well-dressed chap. What's your lay?"

O'Hara sighed. "My *business,*" he said testily, because his head hurt and his pride still pained him and he did not care to stand here discussing events for the rest of the night, "is police work, the same as yours. Fergus O'Hara is the name, an operative of the Pinkerton Agency, Chicago."

Gun and lantern lowered. "You're a *detective?*" the policeman asked, impressed.

"I am—though perhaps not of the caliber of the renowned Mr. Pinkerton, nor of such other of his operatives as Mr. George H. Bangs. Still and again"—dryly—"I have my qualities."

From the inside pocket of his coat he produced his own billfold and extracted the letter from Allan Pinkerton and the Chicago & Eastern Central Railroad pass, both of which identified him, as the bearer of these documents, to be a Pinkerton Police agent. The policeman read both in the lantern light and then returned them to O'Hara. He said respectfully, "What would you be doing way out here in California, Mr. O'Hara?''

''My wife and I are on the trail of a bandit gang that has been terrorizing Adams Express coaches here and in Nevada. We traced them to San Francisco, and we now have reliable information that they're to be found in the Stockton vicinity.''

''Your *wife* is a Pinkerton agent too? A *woman?*''

O'Hara regarded him as if he were a dullard, which he might well have been, and said irritably, ''You've never heard of Miss Kate Warne, one of Mr. Pinkerton's most trusted operatives? No, I don't suppose you have. Well, my wife has no official connection with the agency, but since one of the leaders of this gang is reputed to be a woman, and since my lady has assisted me in the past—women being able to obtain information in places men cannot—I've brought her with me.''

The policeman nodded. ''I'll apologize to you, sir. I had no idea when I saw you here—''

O'Hara waved the rest of it away.

''Well,'' the policemen said, and cleared his throat. Then he seemed to remember his duties. ''Can you describe the man responsible for Stuart's death?''

''Not a bit, I'm afraid. I saw him as no more than a shadow at any time.''

''You say you lost pursuit on the waterfront?''

''Aye.'' O'Hara saw no purpose in mentioning the footpad.

The policeman paused, as if trying to think of something else of relevance to ask. Since he had all the facts he needed, he said finally, ''Well, I guess I have all the facts I'll need. I won't detain you any longer, sir. That's a nasty cut you've got there, and you should have it attended to."

"I'll be doing just that," O'Hara said. "My wife and I are stopping at the Lick House if you'll be needing me further—but I'll thank you, and the gentleman behind you, not to be revealing my name and occupation to anyone, least of all to the newspapers. If the gang learns of a Pinkerton's presence in this area, they'll scatter wide; or worse yet, they'll make an attempt on our lives."

"I understand," the policeman said, and the civilian nodded gravely. "I'll not say a word to anyone."

O'Hara left the alley and started downhill. He walked quickly at first, but because that made his head throb, he slowed his pace. The streets were still very much empty, which suited him. It was his devout hope that the lobby of the Lick House would also be empty when he arrived, and the desk clerk either asleep or out paying a nature call. The prospect of facing Hattie in his present condition was bad enough; he did not care to have anyone else see him.

So, naturally, he reached the entrance to the hotel at exactly the same moment a carriage drew up and disgorged Mr. Horace T. Goatleg.

"Good Lord, sir," the fat man said in surprise. He wrinkled his nose at the pungent, yeasty aroma of O'Hara's clothing. "What's happened to you?"

"Nothing of consequence," O'Hara told him with deliberate sarcasm. "I've only been nearly drowned twice, once by water and once by beer, beaten about the head, shot at, held up by a footpad, and involved in a murder. A typical visitor's evening in San Francisco, no doubt."

Goatleg stared at him. He said, "You're quite serious, aren't you," and he sounded horrified.

"I am."

"But who was murdered?"

"A young man in an alley five blocks distant."

"Killed by the footpad?"

"Not the one who accosted me."

"Well—how could you have nearly been drowned in *beer?*"

"It's all a long story, Mr. Goatleg, and if you don't mind I'd rather not be standing about here for the time it would take to explain it."

"Just as you say. If there is anything I can do—"

"Nothing at all. I'll be saying good night now."

O'Hara turned and entered the hotel before Goatleg could offer a further comment. He knew he was being rude, but he did not particularly care. His head ached malignantly, and his humor was growing fouler by the minute.

The lobby proved to be deserted, but the prim clerk stood in an alert position behind the desk. He cast one look at O'Hara and raised both eyebrows in a superior and disdainful expression. Assuming a pose of righteous disapproval, he made sniffing noises with clear distaste. His eyes said: I *told* you about the Barbary Coast, didn't I?

O'Hara leaned over the desk and said, "Do you know what it is to have intercourse with a passionate whore in a tub of lager?"

The clerk looked at him aghast. Even so, a hint of eager prurience crept into his eyes. Unconsciously he craned forward from the hips like a man awaiting a great and forbidden revelation.

"It's the finest fucking drink a man ever had,"

O'Hara said, and went around and plucked the second of his two room keys from its cubbyhole slot. Leaving the clerk red-faced and spluttering, he climbed the stairs with a perverse and humorless smile bending the corners of his mouth.

There was no light showing beneath the door of his and Hattie's suite, and he breathed a tentative sigh of relief. Carefully he turned the key in the latch, eased the door open, slipped inside, groped his way through the sitting room and into the bedroom on the balls of his feet, and began shrugging quietly out of his Chesterfield.

"Light the lamp, Fergus O'Hara," Hattie's voice said from the bed.

The tone and inflection of those words made O'Hara cringe slightly: they were colder than the foggy night without. "Now, Hattie—" he began.

"You needn't bother pretending, reeking of alcohol as you do."

"I'm not drunk, my lady," he said defensively.

"Then you're the next thing to it."

"I've not had a drink since a single brandy in the Gentlemen's Room after I left you"—which was the whitest of lies.

"How do you explain the way you smell, then?"

"A skalpeen pitched a keg of lager off a brewery wagon at me," O'Hara said. "The keg missed and struck a brick building wall in such a fashion that it broke open and drenched me where I'd fallen."

Hattie said, "Humpf."

"Well, it's the bloody truth," O'Hara said. He stalked to the dressing table, fumbled out a match, and lighted the banquet lamp there. A soft yellow glow filled the room. Hattie sat up in bed, blinked, focused on O'Hara, and then stared at him with her mouth parting; her expression seemed undecided between concern and greater anger.

"So," she said, "not only drunk but in a fight besides."

"I am not drunk!" O'Hara roared, and almost immediately someone in the next room began pounding on the wall. He muttered a dark oath, took off one boot, stumbled over to the wall, and beat on it several times with the heel in retaliation. Then he turned and said again to Hattie, but more quietly this time, "I am not drunk."

"How did you get that cut on your head?"

"I was attacked."

"Attacked by whom?"

He crossed to where their luggage was laid out and opened his banjo case. When he was upset or felt the need for any manner of inner reflection, he invariably picked up the banjo and began strumming it. Which he did now, sitting on one of the room's two velvet-cushioned parlor chairs.

Hattie got out of bed and fetched a basin of water and a clean towel off the lavatory stand. Gingerly she commenced sponging dried blood from the wound on O'Hara's temple. "Well, Fergus?" she said. "I'm waiting."

Scowling, O'Hara picked out the opening bars—not very harmoniously—of "Kathleen Mavourneen," one of his favorite Irish ballads. Then, tersely, he told her everything that had happened to him on this evening—with the exception, that is, of his visits to the Bella Union and the heart of the Barbary Coast.

Hattie did not say anything when he was finished.

After applying to his temple a court plaster from the first-aid supplies in one of her bags, she returned to the bed and sat with her back against the headboard.

O'Hara said, "Don't you believe me?"

"Oh, I believe you."

"It's the truth, and I swear it in the name of St. Pat."

Hattie sighed. "Just once," she said, "it would be pleasant to go somewhere without your getting into some manner of trouble. I never saw such a trouble-gathering man—by profession *and* by nature."

O'Hara decided it would behoove him to remain silent.

"Well," she said resignedly, "at least I've to be thankful you're the luckiest Irishman this side of County Kilkenny. Your wounds heal; some men's don't."

Like Thomas A. Stuart's, O'Hara thought. He finished playing "Kathleen Mavourneen," but he did not feel much better. He put the banjo away, took off his beer-sodden clothing, used the chamber pot, washed in a fresh basin of water, and had two generous pulls on his private bottle. "For the throbbing in my head," he said to Hattie.

She scooted down under the sheets until only the top of her head was showing.

O'Hara blew out the lamp and got into bed beside her. He put his hand on her hip. She slapped it away. Bah! he thought sourly—which expression took in everything in general—and lay there feeling just a bit sorry for himself until he drifted off to sleep.

⊶6⊷

Neither O'Hara's headache nor his disposition had improved when he awoke in the morning. A considerable tot of "medicinal" rye and then breakfast also failed to cure or cheer him. Hattie was mostly silent, although she seldom managed to stay angry at him for any length of time; in any case, she left him alone with his brooding and went to shop in Kearny Street —which meant she intended to make him pay dearly in coin of the realm for last night's misadventure.

He read through the morning papers, looking for mention of the death of Thomas Stuart. The *Daily Alta California* carried a brief account of it on page two in which it was stated that "an employee of a reputable, newly formed San Francisco banking institution was murdered in a most terrible fashion." O'Hara's name was not mentioned: the nervous young policeman and the nervous civilian had kept their promises.

Past noon, after a lengthy bath to eliminate the lingering vestiges of beer aroma from body and hair, he went for a walk in the warm and balmy spring sunshine—the fog had long since burned off—and forced himself not to enter any of the saloons he passed. When the first editions of the afternoon papers appeared, he bought them and took them back to the Lick House. The only one of these that contained an account of the slaying was the *Evening Bulletin*. The story took the form of a front-page editorial:

> *That haunt of the vile and debased, and of all manner of moral pollution, the Barbary Coast, has claimed the life of yet another of our respectable citizens beneath the curtain of its onerous darkness. Thomas A. Stuart, a teller in the California Merchants Bank, was foully murdered last night in one of the evil-smelling alleyways near Pacific Avenue. The anonymous assassin escaped, as is the wont of all such soulless cutthroats, into the loathsome warrens of the waterfront district, where perhaps only the wrathful hand of the Deity shall be able to seek him out for punishment.*
>
> *Mr. Stuart was not a victim of robbery. The dregs of humanity who prey on the innocent in this iniquitous cesspool need little motive for their wanton destruction of lives. They commit their venal acts out of sheer perversion, for they are despicable players in a carnival of slaughter and degradation. If Satan himself should choose to manifest in human guise, it is not to be doubted that he would make such an earthly appearance within these putrid confines.*

The editorial went on from there, in the same morally outraged and Sunday-sermon style, to call for the citizens of San Francisco to rise up against the Barbary Coast and raze it to the ground, so that a wholesome district might be constructed upon the site. O'Hara's name was not mentioned here, either.

He played "Kathleen Mavourneen" six times on the

banjo, had another medicinal drink, and napped for an hour. By the time Hattie returned, laden with purchases, he was beginning to feel almost good-humored again; his headache had become tolerably muted, and his wounded pride also pained him less.

They checked out of the Lick House at three, leaving their luggage to be transported to the *Freebooty* by baggage van. The Embarcadero being only a few blocks distant, as O'Hara now all too well knew, they decided to walk to Long Wharf rather than hire a carriage.

The waterfront looked considerably different by day, if not a great deal more respectable. Rotting storage hulks lay side by side in the offshore mud, slowly sinking into it; a warm breeze carried from them the same sour fishy odor O'Hara remembered from last night. Though the war had closed many shipping lanes, the harbor beyond was dotted with ferries, clipper ships, freighters, and Panama and Pacific steamers.

The area was teeming with activity. Men and horses shuttled cargo in and out of the tumble-down warehouses; the roadways, half plank and half dusty rutted earth, were choked with more men and more horses, as well as mules and freight wagons of all sizes. The plank walks were likewise jammed with people massed together in a swirling sea of color: bearded miners and burly roustabouts and sun-weathered farmers; thick-muscled Kanakas and Filipino farmhands and coolie-hatted Chinese; sharp-eyed merchants and foppish gamblers and bonneted ladies who might have been the wives of prominent citizens or trollops on their way to the goldfields of the Mother Lode. The pace and the din were furious.

At exactly 4:00 P.M. the *Freebooty*—and, O'Hara had learned from the Pettibone Company's brochure, some twenty other steamers—would leave the waterfront for Sacramento, Stockton and points in between.

When Hattie and O'Hara reached Long Wharf, they had their first look at the *Freebooty*. She was an impressive sidewheeler: two hundred and forty-five feet long, with slim, graceful lines and an air of gracious elegance; powered, as were the Mississippi packets O'Hara knew from his youth, by a single-cylindered, walking-beam engine. The long rows of windows running full length both starboard and larboard along her deckhouse, where the Social Hall and Gentlemen's and Dining Saloons and most of the staterooms were located, refracted jewel-like the rays of the afternoon sun. Above, to the stern, was the weather deck, on which could be seen the monitor roof of the main cabin, the gallows frame of the walking beam, and the texas—the last containing the luxury staterooms as well as cabins for the steamer's officers. Some distance forward of the texas was the oblong glassed-in structure of the pilothouse, painted the same well-kept white which set off the neatly mitered panels and pointed slatting of the paddle boxes, and which formed on the housing a gleaming background for the vermilion letters of her name.

The *Freebooty*'s stageplank, set aft to the main deck, was filled with passengers and wagons, and flanked by drays and baggage vans; windlasses, connected with fore-hatches, were lowering the last of the heavy freight into the hold. Along the deck railings, men and women clustered, watching the loading proceedings or waving to friends and relatives or looking over to Pacific and Broadway, where other steamers were preparing for departure.

As Hattie and O'Hara approached the stageplank, O'Hara noticed the green banner he had seen in Portsmouth Plaza last night, and then approximately the same number of Mulrooney Guards. Today all of them wore green felt shamrocks pinned to the lapels of their coats, in honor of the forthcoming St. Patrick's Day, and several were smoking thin long-nine cigars; none of them looked any the worse for the battle with the Rebel supporters and the water hoses of the volunteer fire companies. Nearby sat an accumulation of carpetbags and leather cases—and a massive wooden crate which four of the group were attempting to lift for transportation up the plank, and which appeared to be quite heavy.

"Gentle now, lads," one of the Mulrooneys told the lifters. He was the one wearing the Kossuth hat, apparently their leader. "You'll not want to be dropping that crate and banging it open. You know what'll happen then."

The four men managed to get the crate aloft, grunting, and began to stagger with it to the plank. As they started up, two fierce-looking members of the *Freebooty*'s deck crew came down and blocked their way. One of them said, "Before you go any further, gents, show us your manifest on that box."

The Mulrooney wearing the Kossuth hat stepped up to the plank. "What manifest?" he demanded. "This ain't cargo; it's personal belongings."

"Anything heavy as that pays cargo."

"So now you'll be pulling rules out of a hat, will you?"

"Rules is rules," the deckhand said. "And they apply to Bluebellies same as to other folks."

The Mulrooney Guard's face stained a fiery red. "Bluebellies, is it? You damned Copperhead, I'll pound you up into horsemeat!" And he hit the deckhand on the side of the head and knocked him down.

The second crew member stepped forward and hit the Mulrooney on the side of the head and knocked *him* down.

Another member of the Guards stepped forward and hit the second crewman on the side of the head and knocked *him* down.

The first deckhand got up and the first Mulrooney got up, minus his hat, and began swinging at each other; the second crewman got up and began swinging at the second Mulrooney. The other members of the Guards, shouting encouragement, formed a tight circle around the fighting men. Several of the passengers at the *Freebooty*'s railings began to cheer. And the four men carrying the heavy wooden box struggled with it up the stageplank and hurriedly disappeared among the confusion on the main deck.

Hattie tugged at O'Hara's arm, and reluctantly he let her lead him around the area of battle and up the stageplank as well. But once on deck, he maneuvered her to the rail so that he could watch the balance of the fight.

There was not much more to be seen. Several roustabouts and one of the riverboat's mates hurried onto the landing and broke it up. No one seemed to have been injured in the fairly brief melee, except for the two deckhands, who were both unconscious. The mate wanted to know what had started the trouble, and one of the Mulrooney Guards said he didn't exactly know. The mate seemed undecided as to what to do. Finally concluding that to do nothing at all was the best recourse, he turned up the plank again. Four of the roustabouts carried the crewman up after him, followed by the Mulrooney Guards, who were all now loudly singing "John Brown's Body." A few of the passengers applauded.

Hattie, however, shook her head. "Everywhere we go, there seems to be war trouble."

"Aye, it's a sad business."

"Who do you suppose the Mulrooney Guards are, Fergus?"

"A militia company, I expect—and perhaps a mite too spirited for their own good."

"That is putting it mildly," a voice said behind them.

They turned, and O'Hara saw without much pleasure that it was the gambler, John A. Colfax. "Well, Mr. Colfax," he said, "so you're still another passenger for Stockton, are you?"

"Still another?"

"It appears as if every manjack I've come across in San Francisco is bound for Stockton today on the *Freebooty*. I wouldn't be surprised to see your friend Mr. Tanner on board too."

Colfax chuckled. "As a matter of fact, he is on board. Business in Stockton. There is always a good deal of traffic between the two cities, you know." He looked boldly at Hattie. "Would this be your charming wife, Mr. O'Hara?"

"It would." Not without reluctance, O'Hara introduced them.

Colfax bowed, and Hattie allowed him to take her hand. He seemed to want to hold onto it longer than was required, O'Hara thought, but Hattie freed herself gracefully.

"You were saying about the Mulrooney Guards, Mr. Colfax?" she asked him.

"A militia company, as your husband stated. More or less official, although it seems they would rather engage in fights hereabouts than do their supporting of the Union cause on the battlefields in the East. One of the larger groups, with two companies— one in San Francisco and the other in Stockton. I imagine the San Franciscans are joining the Stocktonians for some sort of celebration."

"Tomorrow is St. Patrick's Day," O'Hara said.

"Ah yes, of course."

"You seem to know quite a bit about these Mulrooneys."

"In my business, the more a man knows, the better off he is." Colfax smiled enigmatically. "My eyes and my ears are always open."

Hattie said, "What did the Mulrooneys have in that crate, I wonder?"

Colfax told her he was afraid he couldn't answer that particular question. He seemed about to say something further, but some sort of activity on the landing, where the last of the passengers and cargo were being loaded, caught and held his attention. O'Hara turned, peering out, and saw three closely grouped men hurrying toward the stageplank. The one in the middle, wearing a broadcloth suit, had a nervous, harried expression; cradled in both hands against his body was a large and seemingly heavy black valise.

The two men on either side were more roughly dressed and carried Colt revolvers holstered at their hips. Their hands hovered over the butts, and their eyes scanned the crowd without seeming to do so.

O'Hara frowned and glanced at Colfax. The gambler stood in a posture of interest, shuffling several of the bronze, war-issue cent pieces in his left hand, as he had the previous night at the Lick House. He watched the trio climb the plank, pass near them, and hurry up the aft stairway to the upper decks; then, languidly, he regarded the O'Haras again and touched his hat, a black and flashy plug.

"A pleasure meeting you, Mrs. O'Hara," he said to Hattie. Then he nodded to Fergus and moved away along the rail, disappearing forward.

Hattie looked at O'Hara inquiringly.

He said, "Gold."

"Gold, Fergus?"

"That nervous chap had the look of a banker, and the other two of deputies. A bank transfer of gold specie, or perhaps dust, from San Francisco to Stockton—or so I'm thinking."

"I had the idea gold was shipped mostly by stage out here."

"I expect that's the case," O'Hara said. "It's quicker by steamboat, though, in the case of emergency."

"Where do you imagine they'll keep it?"

"The purser's office, like as not—or the pilothouse."

The three men appeared on the stairway again and crossed to the stageplank; the one in the broadcloth suit looked considerably less nervous, and the other two, walking with their arms swinging freely, no longer seemed interested in the activities of those nearby. O'Hara watched them until they were out of sight.

Hattie said then, "Where did you happen to encounter Mr. Colfax?"

"In the Gentlemen's Room at the Lick House last evening."

"He's a gambler, isn't he?"

"He is."

"He also has an impertinent eye, if you take my meaning."

"I do," O'Hara said, and lowered his eyes impertinently to the front of her dress.

She poked him in the ribs. "I don't like him, Fergus."

"Well, he's a slick lad, even for a gambler. You'd not want to be giving him a specie to put in a village poor box."

"He seemed quite interested in the delivery of gold, if that's what it was."

"So he did," O'Hara said. "So he did."

7

The *Freebooty*'s stageplank was raised at exactly four o'clock, and her buckets immediately began to churn the water in a steady rhythm. Her whistle, which had been shrilling an all-aboard and all-visitors-ashore warning, altered cadence to become a steerage signal for the pilot. All up and down the waterfront now, other whistles sounded and bells clanged and packets commenced backing down from their landings. The adjacent waters of the bay took on a bedlamatic appearance as boats, flags flying from their jackstaffs and from their verge-staffs astern, maneuvered and fought for right of way. Columns of smoke filled the sky, creating a sooty eclipse of the sun.

Hattie and O'Hara stood with other passengers at the hammock-netted larboard railing on the weather deck, opposite the texas. They had come up just prior to departure, had given their tickets to a Chinese steward, and had been shown to their stateroom, the entrance to which was located inside a tunnel-like hallway down the center of the texas. (The cabin, with windows that faced larboard, had carved rosewood paneling, ogee molding, red plush upholstery, and polished brass lamps; it reminded O'Hara nostalgically of a bordello he had had occasion to visit in Saint Louis before meeting Hattie.) Leaving their baggage locked inside, they had come back out on deck.

When the steamer was well clear of the wharves and of other riverboats, her speed increased steadily. She passed near Fort Alcatraz, with its belt of encircling batteries and garrison of soldiers ready to repel any attacks by Rebel privateers who might make their way into Northern waters to prey on Union shipping. Her course, according to the Pettibone brochure, would be north into San Pablo Bay, then east into the narrow Carquinez Straits, then southeast into the San Joaquin River and its winding expanse through the myriad islands of the Delta country. Most of the packets would make stops along the way at small settlements and inhabited islands, but the *Freebooty* would travel uninterrupted directly to Stockton.

Shading her eyes, Hattie looked back with an air of fascination toward the receding skyline of San Francisco. Bathed in light from the sinking sun, the city's hills had the look of great mounds of burnished gold—or so she said to O'Hara.

He said, "You've a poetic soul, my lady."

"Blarney," Hattie told him, but her smile said she was pleased by the remark.

They remained at the rail until the *Freebooty* had passed San Pablo Point, and then O'Hara suggested they acquaint themselves with the packet. He was thinking, more specifically, of acquainting himself with the liquor buffet in the Gentlemen's Saloon.

Two men reached the forward stairway just as

they did, from the direction of the pilothouse. One was the chief pilot, Mr. Woodman—the steamer, at this untroubled point in the journey, would be in the hands of an apprentice or junior pilot—and the other was the bushy-haired mustached man who had been with Woodman in the Bella Union the previous evening. If the pilot was suffering a hangover today, he showed no signs of it; his companion, on the other hand, looked as though he wished he were lying down in a dark room. They preceded Hattie and O'Hara down to the deckhouse.

There were a number of passengers sitting alone or in groups at sun tables near the starboard rail, and others standing along the rail itself. Among these last, O'Hara noticed, was the red-shirted miner from the queue yesterday at the Pettibone offices. And perched on his shoulder, again facing the rear and looking more like a gaily painted vulture, was the same large parrot.

The parrot's attention appeared fixed on something directly across the deck at one of the tables. When the O'Haras were ten paces away, the bird suddenly swooped off the miner's shoulder—the miner took no notice—and flew to a table on top of which reposed an elegant metal cage with a frilly nightcloth rolled up at the top. Inside the cage was a white cockatoo, sitting daintily on a wooden perch. As soon as the parrot landed in front of the cage door, however, the cockatoo made a startled noise and began shaking its feathered head and wings.

Abruptly, leering glassy-eyed at the other bird, the parrot leaped on the cage and shook and snapped at the bars as though to force admittance. "Spread those legs, missie!" it screeched. "Spread those legs, missie!"

Some of the passengers looked shocked, while others, O'Hara included, managed for the sake of propriety to conceal their amusement. The cockatoo, meanwhile, was shrieking in terror. A fat woman in a yellow bonnet who had been conversing at a nearby table wheeled toward the cage and promptly emitted a sound similar to that made by the cockatoo. She began beating at the parrot with her parasol. Looking aggrieved, it released its grip on the cage and flew up onto the weather deck railing, from where it glared down malevolently and sneered at her in what sounded strangely enough like Chinese.

The fat woman rolled the nightcloth down over the cage and its nearly raped cockatoo and stalked off with it in high outrage. Once she had disappeared aft, the parrot stopped sneering in Chinese and flew down from the railing and settled again onto the miner's shoulder.

"Give me a whore anytime," it muttered.

Hattie pretended not to have heard that as O'Hara, grinning, walked her by and down through the entrance doors to the Social Hall. It was a large enclosure, divided into three parts: a central lounge, the Gentlemen's Saloon forward, and the Ladies' Cabin aft. The central lounge was crowded and noisy; tables of food and sweets were arranged along the larboard bulkhead. O'Hara's attention wandered to the Saloon doors, while Hattie's was on the entrance to the Ladies' Cabin.

"I believe I'll see what appointments the *Freebooty* accords us," she said at length. She cocked an eye at O'Hara. "While you're in the Saloon, I'll expect you to stay away from the liquor buffet."

She had a fair uncanny knack at times for reading his mind, O'Hara thought ruefully. He said, "Now, Hattie . . ."

"You had a healthy nip from that bottle of yours before we left the Lick House. That should be sufficient until mealtime."

"Ordinarily it would," O'Hara said. "But my head still hurts, you know, and this fine sea air has honed my thirst to a fine edge—"

"You can quench it with fruit juice or sarsparilla."

O'Hara shuddered. "Sarsparilla," he said.

Hattie said she would see him back in their stateroom shortly, and walked away to the Ladies' Cabin. O'Hara looked at the doors to the Saloon and concluded there was no point in visiting the premises without purpose; it would be looking temptation too squarely in the eye. He departed the Social Hall instead and walked down to the main deck.

There, in the open areas and in the shedlike expanse beneath the superstructures, deck passengers and cargo were pressed together in noisy confusion: men and women and children, wagons and animals and chickens in coops, sacks, bales, boxes, hogsheads, cords of bull pine for the roaring fireboxes under the boilers. And, too, the Mulrooney Guards, who were loosely grouped near the taffrail, alternately singing such Irish ballads as "The Girl I Left Behind Me" and passing around earthenware jugs.

O'Hara sauntered near the group, stood with his back against a stanchion, and began to shave cuttings from his tobacco plug into his briar. One of the nearest Mulrooneys—small and fair and feisty-looking—

noticed O'Hara, studied his luxuriant red beard, and then approached him carrying one of the jugs. Without preamble he demanded to know if Fergus was Irish.

"I am," O'Hara said with pride and dignity.

The Mulrooney Guard slapped him on the back. "I knew it!" he said effusively. "My name's Billy Culligan. Have a drap of the crature."

Which meant that the contents of the job was poteen—a powerful colorless homemade Irish whisky fashioned from barley, oats, sugar and yeast. O'Hara ran his tongue over his lips, and after a brief deliberation decided Hattie had told him only to stay away from the buffet; there was no deceit in accepting hospitality from fellows of the Auld Sod, now was there? He took the jug, wiped the mouth, and drank deeply. Culligan watched him with approval.

When O'Hara lowered the jug he grinned at the Mulrooney and said, "'Tis, a fine crature, indeed." Then he introduced himself and told Billy Culligan he and his missus were traveling to Stockton on a business matter.

"You won't be conducting business tomorrow, now, will you?"

"On St. Pat's Day?" O'Hara was properly shocked.

"Boyo, I like you," Culligan said. "I do for a fact. How would you be wanting to join in on the biggest St. Pat's Day celebration in the entire sovereign state of California?"

"I'd be liking nothing better."

"Then come to Green Park, on the north of Stockton, 'twixt nine and ten and tell the lads you're a friend of Billy Culligan. There'll be a parade, and all the food you can eat, and all the liquor you can drink. Oh, it'll be a fine celebration, boyo.''

O'Hara said he and the missus would be there, meaning it. Culligan offered another drink, which O'Hara readily accepted; then the little Mulrooney stepped closer and said in a conspiratorial voice, ''Come round here to the taffrail just before we come a-steaming into Stockton on the morrow. We've a plan to start off St. Pat's Day with a mighty salute—part of the reason we sent our own wives and families on the *San Joaquin* instead of bringing 'em along on the *Freebooty*—and you won't want to be missing out on that, either.'' He laughed boisterously, winked at O'Hara, and took his jug away into the midst of the other Guards.

O'Hara pondered this last for a moment, but its significance escaped him. He shrugged and decided he would find it out in the morning. By and by, when he had finished his pipe, he returned to the deckhouse, entered the Social Hall's central lounge, helped himself to a handful of mints, and then, with a breath to match his conscience, went up to the texas to his and Hattie's stateroom.

8

The Dining Saloon, which Hattie and O'Hara repaired to shortly after seven, offered no view except for that of closed stateroom doors, since it was located in the wide lamplit "tunnel" which bisected the forward section of the deckhouse lengthwise; but atmosphere, as O'Hara knew from his travels on the Mississippi, was unnecessary in the face of a steamboat repast. Linen-covered long tables, tended by Chinese and Negro waiters, were half-filled with early diners. At the Captain's Table aft were the graying, leather-featured captain, the chief pilot, Woodman, and a third, uniformed officer who like as not was the *Freebooty*'s purser.

O'Hara took chairs for them at the forward end. Almost immediately a waiter appeared with a tray of relishes and the meal began. For the next hour O'Hara, who had a fondness for fine food nearly equal to his fondness for spirits, indulged himself lustily: huge raw oysters, fresh lobster, venison, potatoes, half a dozen different vegetables, and strong California red wine as well as light French white. Even Hattie, who was always conscious of her figure, sampled a little of everything.

When O'Hara finally pushed his plate away, he sighed serenely and began packing his pipe. As he fitted the stem between his teeth, he saw Horace T. Goatleg and Charles Tanner enter the Dining Saloon—the first he had seen of either of them on board the riverboat.

The pair threaded their way between the rows of tables, noticed the O'Haras, and came around to where they were sitting. Goatleg wore expensive black broadcloth tonight, as well as a ruffled linen shirt with a pointed collar; Tanner was dressed in the same sack coat, nankeen trousers, black eyepatch and diffident manner of last evening.

O'Hara performed introductions: Goatleg bowed and Tanner blinked his good eye and Hattie stared at Tanner's eyepatch until she realized she was being impolite; then she lowered her gaze and fussed with the sleeves of her paletot. The moment the two men sat down, the waiter appeared with the relish tray. In deference to the new diners, O'Hara reluctantly put his pipe away.

"Well, sir," Goatleg said as he speared a pickle with his fork, "how are you feeling after your misadventure last night?"

"Sorry that it happened," O'Hara said shortly.

Tanner asked, "What misadventure is this?"

"The shooting of a young man near the Barbary Coast." Goatleg began to generously spread peach preserves on a wedge of bread. "There was mention of it in today's newspapers."

"Ah," Tanner said, and looked expectantly at O'Hara.

Who grimaced, because he had no desire to enter into an explanation of events for the one-eyed man's and Goatleg's benefit. "I was drawn into an unsuccessful chase of the murderer by proximity to the crime, nothing more." He said it with finality.

Tanner, however, seemed to want to pursue the subject. "Curious that you should find yourself mixed in with a Barbary Coast murder on your first night in San Francisco."

"How d'you mean, curious?"

"Oh, I meant no offense. Just seemed curious, is all."

No more curious, O'Hara thought, then your following me from the Lick House to Portsmouth Plaza, and then rushing off when I chanced to notice you. But he decided not to say anything about that incident, at least not at the moment. Perhaps later, should he happen to encounter Tanner in more private circumstances. Instead he said, "I was fortunate to be escaping with my life, which makes me a bit reluctant to discuss the matter. You understand, I'm sure."

"Of course," Goatleg said. "Certainly."

Tanner—apparently a man given to abruptly shifting moods—lowered his gaze to his hands, stroked his eyepatch, and otherwise looked newly dead for the second time since O'Hara had met him.

The waiter brought thick slabs of roast beef for Tanner and Goatleg, coffee for the O'Haras. The fat man ate in large mouthfuls, with great gusto; Tanner, on the other hand, kept his eye on his plate and picked at his food in a kind of desultory, furtive manner, as though he were performing an illegal, immoral and unnatural act—one he was not even enjoying.

At length Goatleg said to O'Hara, "What is your opinion of the new draft law?"

"That it shows the wisdom of Mr. President Lincoln," O'Hara answered. "The Union can't be winning the war without an inexhaustible supply of troops."

Tanner looked up—another mood change—and said argumentatively, "The Union can't win the war at all, as far as I'm concerned. When the final battle is won, the Confederacy will have persevered."

"D'you really think that, Mr. Tanner?"

"I damned well do."

"You have Southern leanings, then?"

"I have ties with the South—strong ties."

"It seems we all three do. But leanings are another matter."

"*Your* leanings are to the Union, I take it."

"They are," O'Hara said. "My beliefs won't allow otherwise, despite the location of my birth and boyhood."

The one-eyed man glared at him with one eye, and Goatleg, seeming to sense the development of a small but potentially volatile undercurrent of hostility, cleared his throat in a pointed way. "Perhaps I shouldn't have broached the subject of war here at the supper table; it does have a way of replacing appetite with unserviceable zeal, doesn't it?"

O'Hara saw that Hattie appeared uncomfortable, and divined no good purpose in continuing the conversation. "You're right in that," he said to Goatleg, and gained his feet. "If you'll excuse us now, gentlemen, we'll be digesting our meal with an after-supper stroll about the decks."

"Oh, indeed." Then, as though to reestablish an atmosphere of good humor, the fat man said, "An excellent meal demands the proper digestion—so one may follow it not too much later with yet another excellent meal."

While he rumbled again, Tanner managed once more to simulate a corpse.

O'Hara said "Aye" and "Good evening," and took Hattie's arm and guided her out of the Dining Saloon.

She said then, "I can't say as I approve of the acquaintances you seem to be making of late, Fergus. Particularly that Mr. Tanner."

"I can't say as I do either," he told her.

"What happened to his eye?"

"I didn't warrant it was proper to be asking him."

She shivered. "Perhaps it's best if we don't know."

"Mm, perhaps it is."

They went aft along the starboard rail. The decks were filled with other strolling or seated passengers, owing to the fact that it was a fine evening: mild, with little breeze and no sign of the thick tule fog that doubtless made Northern California riverboating a hazardous prospect at certain times of the year. The *Freebooty*—aglow with hundreds of lights—had come through the Carquinez Straits, passed Chipp's Island, and was now entering the San Joaquin River. A pale gold full moon silvered the slow-moving water and turned a ghostly white the long stretches of fields on both sides of the river, the willows and tangles of wild grape and mistletoe-festooned cottonwoods which grew thickly along the banks.

Hattie and O'Hara made a complete circuit of the deckhouse, then went up to the weather deck, past the gallows frame of the walking-beam engine. Through the vent opening they could hear the *Ssoo, hah! Ssoo, hah!* of the steam-driven piston, smell the sharpness of cylinder oil. They walked forward of the texas and stood close together at the larboard rail, not far from the palely lantern-lit pilothouse. That area was presently deserted, and the evening was so still that the only sound was the soft chunking of the paddle boxes.

They had been there for a minute or two when they heard footsteps and turned to see the captain and the chief pilot, Woodman, returning from supper. Touching the visor of his cap, the graying master wished them good evening; the pilot merely grunted. Then they were past and moving toward the pilothouse.

A nightbird cried out from somewhere close by, among the trees along the levee, and Hattie edged closer. O'Hara smiled and started to put his arm around her shoulders—and an explosive, angry cry came from the pilothouse, startling them both. This was followed by muffled voices, another sharp exclamation, movement not clearly perceived through the window glass and beyond partially drawn rear curtains, and several sharp blasts on the pilot whistle.

Natural curiosity took O'Hara away from the rail, hurrying; Hattie was close behind him. The door to the pilothouse stood open when they reached it, and O'Hara turned inside by one step. The enclosure was almost as opulent as their stateroom: the curtains of red and gold cloth, a red plush sofa, two shiny brass cuspidors, new oilcloth on the floor, a blackened winter stove, brass bell and whistle knobs, and a huge, polished-wood wheel directly in front of a high-backed leather seat on which the pilot would sit. But O'Hara saw all of this only peripherally. What captured his full attention was three men now grouped before the wheel, and the four items on the floor close to and against the starboard bulkhead.

Woodman stood clutching two of the wheel spokes, red-faced with anger, and the captain was bending over the kneeling figure of the third man—the same round-faced young blond individual who had completed the trio with Woodman and the bushy-haired man at the Bella Union. The young blond wore a buttoned-up sack coat and baggy trousers, both of which were grit-streaked from the dusty/sooty oil-cloth. He held the back of his head cupped in one palm as he made soft moaning sounds.

One of the items on the floor was a steel pry bar. The others were a small safe bolted to the bulkhead, a black valise—the one O'Hara had seen carried about by the nervous man and his two bodyguards in San Francisco—and a medium-sized iron strongbox, just large enough to have fit inside the valise. The safe door, minus its combination dial, stood wide open; the valise and the strongbox were open as well.

And all three were quite obviously empty.

∽9∽

Woodman jerked the bell knobs, signaling an urgent request for a lessening of speed, and began barking stand-by orders into a speaking tube that would be connected with the engine room. Then, still holding firmly onto the wheel, he opened the glass windshield on its outward hinges and put his head out and bellowed for the watchman on the forecastle below to give him an immediate sounding. He kept his head outside, moving it to and fro, checking the *Freebooty*'s position in relation to the familiar path of the river.

The captain was saying, "It's a miracle we haven't drifted far enough out of the channel to run afoul of a snag or a bar—a miracle, Bradley."

Bradley, the young blond man and doubtless a junior pilot, said defensively, "I can't be held to blame sir. Whoever it was hit me from behind. I was sitting at the wheel when I heard the door open, and I thought it was you and Mr. Woodman returning from your supper, so I didn't bother to turn about. The next thing, my head seemed to explode, and I don't recall a single thing until you shook me just a moment ago.''

He managed to regain his feet and moved stiffly to the red plush sofa, hitching up his loose trousers with one hand; the other still held the back of his head. Woodman spun the wheel a half-turn to larboard, then pulled back inside; as he did so, he glanced over his shoulder and saw O'Hara and Hattie. His eyes narrowed. ''Get out of here!'' he shouted. ''There's nothing here for you.''

''Perhaps, now, that isn't true,'' O'Hara said mildly. His own eyes were bright with interest. ''You've had a robbery, haven't you?''

''That is none of your affair.''

A shout from the watchman snapped Woodman's head around: ''Quarter less three!'' Which meant the river depth here was sixteen and a half feet.

''Quarter less three!'' Woodman echoed, and spun the wheel another half-turn to larboard.

''Mark three!'' the watchman called. Eighteen feet.

''Mark three!'' There was relief in Woodman's answer this time. He relaxed his grip on the wheel and yanked the bell knobs again, now in the all-clear signal. The steamer's speed, which had slackened noticeably, soon increased again.

While all this was going on, O'Hara had come boldly forward and motioned Hattie to shut the pilothouse door. She had done so. When Woodman next glanced around and saw O'Hara standing less than ten paces away, he yelled, ''I told you to get out of here! Who do you think you are?''

''Fergus O'Hara—an operative of the Pinkerton Police Agency.''

Woodman stared at him, open-mouthed. The captain and Bradley had given their attention to him as well, looking just as surprised. At length, in a softer tone, the pilot said, "Pinkerton Agency?"

"Of Chicago, Illinois; Allan Pinkerton, Principal."

O'Hara produced his billfold, extracted the letter of introduction and railroad pass, and handed them to the captain. The captain studied them for a moment, gave them over to Woodman. Meanwhile, O'Hara explained about his and Hattie's being on the trail of the bandit gang that had been terrorizing Adams Express coaches and which was now reputed to be found in the Stockton area.

Woodman handed the identification back to him. "Well, we can surely use a trained detective after what has happened here."

O'Hara nodded shortly. "Is it gold you've had stolen?"

"Gold—yes. How did you know that?"

He told them of witnessing the delivery of the valise at Long Wharf. He asked then, "How large an amount is involved?"

"Forty thousand dollars," the captain said.

"That's a fair considerable sum."

"To state it mildly, Mr. O'Hara."

"Was it specie or dust?"

"Dust. An urgent consignment from the California Merchants Bank to their branch in Stockton."

O'Hara scowled. "California Merchants Bank, did you say?"

"Yes."

The scowl deepened. Now, that was an interesting fact, when coupled with another: the man who had been murdered in the alleyway last night, Thomas Stuart, had been an employee of the California Merchants Bank. Coincidence—or was there some connection between the shooting of Stuart and the theft of the gold shipment?

O'Hara said, "How many men had foreknowledge of the consignment?"

"The officials of the bank and of the Pettibone Company. The request was received yesterday, and the decision made then to ship on the *Freebooty*."

"When were Mr. Woodman and yourself informed of this decision?"

"Today at noon."

"Were any other officers of the packet told?"

"Only the purser, Mr. Flucke."

"This young lad here, Bradley?"

"No sir," the junior pilot said. "I knew nothing about it until just a few moments ago."

"Would you be telling me, Captain, who was present when the delivery was made this afternoon?"

"Mr. Woodman and myself, and a friend of his visiting in San Francisco—a newspaperman."

The tall man with the bushy hair and mustache, O'Hara thought. "Can you be vouching for this newspaperman?" he asked Woodman.

"I can. His reputation is unimpeachable. If it were not, I wouldn't have invited him to visit with us as he chose when I learned he was making the trip to Stockton."

"Has anyone other than he been here in the pilothouse?"

"Not to my knowledge," the captain said.

Bradley said, "No one came by while I was here alone."

"None of you noticed anyone shirking about at any time?"

None of them had.

"Do you usually keep such shipments in the safe here?"

"Yes," the captain said. "Sometimes we do place consignments in the purser's safe, but it was determined to use the safe here"—he made a wry face—"because it was felt this safe was the sturdier of the two."

"Who made this determination?"

"Mr. Pettibone, Junior, and myself."

"It appears as though almost any man on board could be the culprit," Woodman said sourly. "Just how do you propose to find out which one, O'Hara?"

O'Hara did not reply. He bent to examine the safe. It was of Wells Fargo manufacture and seemed as well constructed as any; the combination dial appeared to have been snapped off, however, by a hand with experience at such villainous business. The valise and the strongbox had also been forced with a minimum of labor. The pry bar was an ordinary tool and had doubtless also been the weapon used to knock Bradley unconscious.

He began moving about the interior of the pilothouse, studying each fixture. He bowed his waist and waddled back and forth staring at the oilcloth floor and looking for all the world like a man engaged in a drunken imitation of a penguin. (An individual in Saint Louis had once made the mistake of saying this very same thing to O'Hara's face after he had dropped a five-dollar gold piece in a saloon and gone waddling around the room looking for it—a mistake which led to a sorry day for the individual, O'Hara, the saloon, a half-dozen Osage Indians, two borrowed keelboats, and a riverside revival meeting presided over by a fundamentalist hellfire-and-brimstone preacher. But that is another story.)

Finally, O'Hara got down on hands and knees and peered under the winter stove and under the red plush sofa, once Bradley had stood and moved shakily aside. And it was under the sofa that he found the coin.

His sweeping fingers touched it, grasped it, and closed it into his palm. Standing again, he glanced at the coin and saw that it was made of bronze, a small war-issue cent piece shinily new and free of sooty dust, such as it would have acquired had it been under the sofa for any length of time. A grim smile stretched the edges of his mouth as he slipped the coin into his vest pocket.

Woodman said, "Did you find something?"

"Perhaps. Then again, perhaps not."

When O'Hara came forward again, the captain gave him a willful, duty-in-the-face-of-adversity look. "As master of the *Freebooty*," he said, "I am responsible for the gold. It would be cowardly to place the task of investigating its theft solely in the hands of another—even a Pinkerton policeman. We'll both make inquiries."

"Aye," O'Hara agreed, "but discreetly. It wouldn't do to have the whole packet aware of the robbery."

The captain nodded. "One thing I can do more easily than you is to question the texas stewards and passengers. There is a chance one of them might have seen the thief."

"Just as you think best," O'Hara said. "I've

another direction which I'll be wanting to pursue for the time being.''

Moments later, he and Hattie left the pilothouse and walked rapidly along the larboard rail to the texas. Hattie said then, the first words she had spoken in the past twenty minutes, ''Fergus, I expect you're making a mistake involving yourself in this gold thievery. It's none of our concern—''

''You're wrong there, my lady,'' O'Hara said. ''It just may be that the robbery is connected with the murder of Mr. Stuart last night—and therefore with the skalpeen who struck me down and attempted to take my own life.''

Hattie was incredulous. ''How in heaven's name is that possible?''

He explained about Stuart's having been an employee of the California Merchants Bank.

''Coincidence; nothing more,'' she said.

''My inclusion in the events of Stuart's murder, aye. But as for what's happened here tonight, perhaps it's more the benevolence of St. Pat himself—granting me the opportunity for sweet retribution after all, not to mention the opportunity for the recovering of forty thousand in missing gold.''

''The only opportunity I see,'' Hattie said gloomily, ''is for more trouble.''

''Hattie, when it comes to business matters, you'll have to admit I'm generally knowing what's best.'' He gave her a thin smile. ''Besides that, what would Allan Pinkerton be saying if I simply passed by my duty as well as all these fine fair fields?''

''But—''

''No buts; my mind's made up,'' O'Hara said.

They had reached the door to their stateroom, and he patted her cheek perfunctorily by way of parting (and missed seeing the malicious glare that gesture netted him). His eyes glittered. "I've an investigation to commence."

⊶10⊷

The Gentlemen's Saloon was a long room with a liquor buffet at one end and private tables and card layouts spread throughout, most of which were occupied by professional gamblers engaged in fleecing unsuspecting citizens at such sporting games as poker, blackjack and chuck-a-luck. There were also Chinese waiters, dozens of sparkling brass cuspidors, a hundred or more men speaking in loud, sometimes profane voices, and a pall of cigar smoke that had the thick consistency of tule fog.

Roaming the room, O'Hara finally located the shrewd, handsome features of John A. Colfax at a table in a far corner. Three other men sat at the same table: Charles Tanner, the bushy-haired newspaperman friend of Woodman's, and the red-shirted miner who owned, and on whose shoulder inevitably sat, the large and basilisk-eyed parrot. They were playing draw poker, and not surprisingly most of the stakes —gold nuggets and a few greenbacks—rested in front of Colfax.

With feigned nonchalance, O'Hara approached the table and stopped to the right of the newspaperman—just as Colfax took the current pot with four treys.

"Son of a bitch," the miner said.

"Son of a bitch," the parrot agreed.

They both glared malignantly at the gambler.

O'Hara said, "Good evening, gentlemen."

The four men looked up at him. Tanner sucked what was probably a hoarhound drop and stroked his eyepatch, and Colfax smiled unctuously. "Well, O'Hara," he said, "are you and your charming wife enjoying the voyage thus far?"

"We are. You seem to be enjoying it, too, judging from that stack of legal tender in front of you."

"I *have* had a fortunate evening so far, yes."

"Goddamned right you have," the miner said in a grumbling voice. "You've been taking my money for three solid hours now."

O'Hara said, "Three solid hours?"

"Since just after we met at the bar."

"You've been playing without pause since then?"

"Mr. Morrison and I have," the newspaperman said. Through tendrils of smoke from his cigar, he studied O'Hara with mild blue eyes. "Mr. Tanner joined us a few minutes past."

Tanner said, "Why do you ask, O'Hara?"

"Oh, I was thinking I saw Mr. Colfax up on the weather deck—just about an hour ago, it was, forward of the texas."

"I'm afraid you were mistaken," Colfax said. Now that the poker game had been momentarily suspended, he had once more produced the handful of war-issue coins and begun to toy with them.

"You haven't left the table, then, since you began playing?" O'Hara asked casually.

"Once, about an hour ago, as a matter of fact; but only for fifteen minutes or so, to use the lavatory." The gambler's smile grew more unctuous. "You're a very inquisitive man, Mr. O'Hara."

The parrot, which had transferred its stare to Fergus, took this opportunity to make a rudely flatulent noise—as though it remembered him from the Pettibone offices in San Francisco. O'Hara ignored it. He said to Colfax, "I was sure it was you I was seeing on the weather deck, is all."

Colfax shrugged with apparent indifference. "I haven't been on the weather deck at all this trip," he said.

Tanner's one good eye was fixed on O'Hara with probing interest; the newspaperman's gaze contained curiosity as well. O'Hara decided it would be wise to drop the matter for the present. He pretended to be aware for the first time of the one-cent pieces the gambler was shuffling. "Lucky coins, Mr. Colfax?" he asked.

Colfax seemed faintly surprised by the question. He glanced at the coins in his hand, then back at O'Hara again. "These? Why yes, something of the sort. I obtained a sackful of them on a wager once, and my luck has been quite phenomenal ever since. I am superstitious about such things."

"You don't see many coins like that in California."

"No, they're practically worthless out here. In fact, I've noticed their being used to decorate some types of leather goods."

The miner said irritably, "To hell with lucky coins. Are we playing poker or ain't we?"

"Of course," Colfax said. He slipped the war-issue cents into a pocket of his Prince Albert and reached for the deck of cards. His interest in O'Hara appeared to have waned.

When Tanner put another hoarhound drop into his mouth, the parrot leaned toward him and fluffed its wings and looked both baleful and demanding. Absently Tanner gave it one of the candies, which it loudly crunched and swallowed; then it made the flatulent noise again and said, "Goddamned Chink," a comment not only ungrateful but inaccurate. The one-eyed man, meanwhile, gave O'Hara a final glance and then, with apparent reluctance, turned back to the game. The newspaperman, shrugging, followed suit.

There was little for O'Hara to do then except to retreat. He recrossed the smoke-filled room and approached the buffet. A bartender with a splendid handlebar mustache brought him a pony of rye, and O'Hara rotated the glass on the mahogany surface of the bar, cogitating.

Colfax might well be his man—there was the war-issue coin from under the pilothouse sofa, and the fact that the gambler had left the poker game at about the time of the robbery—and yet, his mind was full of nagging doubts now. For one thing, what could Colfax have done with the gold? The weight of forty thousand in dust was considerable, and he could not very well carry it in his pockets. He had said he was gone from the table for only "fifteen minutes or so," which was sufficient time for him to have committed the theft and returned to the Saloon, but precious little time for him to have hidden the gold. O'Hara had already considered and rejected the possibility that the miner and the

— 92 —

newspaperman were accomplices; a conjoinment of three men was hardly necessary for a successful assault on the pilothouse.

There were other factors too. One: gentlemen gamblers made considerable sums of money by preying on the foibles of honest men; they seldom found it necessary to resort to baser thievery. Two: how could Colfax, while sitting here in the Saloon, have known when only one man would be present in the pilothouse? It was improbable that the captain and Woodman ate supper at precisely the same time during each voyage. A different, unknown accomplice might have observed the situation and signaled Colfax somehow; but if there really was a confederate, why hadn't he done the robbery himself?

O'Hara scowled, tossed down the rye without his usual enjoyment, and ordered another. If Colfax was not the culprit, confound it, the list of possible suspects included every manjack on board the *Freebooty*.

He considered. The fact of the war-issue coin still bothered him; perhaps it had no significance at all, but he was inclined—he had always trusted his instincts—to believe differently. But if not to Colfax, to whom did it point? Answer: to no one, and to everyone. Even though war-issue cent pieces were uncommon in California, at least a dozen men presently on board the steamer might have one or two in their pockets.

A remark the gambler had made came to mind, then: such coins were used to decorate some types of leather goods. Aye, that was yet another possibility, he thought. If the guilty man had been wearing a holster or a vest or some other article adorned with the cent pieces, one might well have popped loose from its fastenings, unnoticed in the tenseness of the robbery.

O'Hara slid the found coin from his pocket and examined it carefully. There were small scratches on its surface which might have been made by stud fasteners, but he could not be sure. The scratches might also have resulted from any of a hundred other means—and the cent could still belong to John A. Colfax.

He turned his reflection to the potential link between the murder of Thomas Stuart and the fact that the stolen gold had come from the same banking institution that had employed Stuart. If not a coincidence, one possible explanation was that Stuart had been in league with the thief and had supplied to him the information that the shipment of gold was being made on this voyage of the packet. Perhaps the two had had a falling-out, or Stuart had been a mere pawn from the beginning and the bullet had been used to sever the partnership.

But the death of the bank employee offered no clue to the identity of the robber, potential connection or not. And neither had any of these ruminations. Nor would they, it seemed, without more information.

O'Hara finished his second rye, left the Saloon and the Social Hall, and stood for a moment at the larboard rail, looking out at the silvery landscape beyond the river levee while he debated his next move. He settled on a consultation with the purser, Mr. Flucke, and started aft toward the stairway.

Someone behind him said, "Mr. O'Hara."

He stopped, turning. It was Charles Tanner.

The one-eyed man came up to him. "I'd like a few words with you, if you don't mind."

O'Hara shrugged. "What is it you're wanting to discuss?"

"Your interest in Colfax's whereabouts an hour or so ago. The questions you asked struck me as anything but casual ones."

"Did they, now? And just what would *your* interest be in the matter?"

"Perhaps none, perhaps a great deal," Tanner said. His manner, O'Hara thought, had altered markedly. He was no longer mild-mannered and diffident; there was a flinty hardness in his face and in his voice. "Did something happen on the weather deck tonight? Something which might involve Colfax?"

"Nothing of consequence."

"Suppose you allow me to judge that."

"Suppose you tell me why you should be so interested."

"I have my reasons. What happened on the weather deck?"

O'Hara manufactured a smile. "I don't have anything to tell you, Mr. Tanner."

"Was someone else besides Colfax involved?"

"Such as who?"

"I insist on an answer, O'Hara."

"I told you, I've nothing to be telling you. Perhaps you might ask the captain, or one of the other officers. If there was an occurrence tonight, they'd be the ones to relate it to you—if they're of a mind to."

Tanner leaned toward him slightly, anger flattening his lips together; even though he kept his hands at his sides, the aspect he presented was almost menacing. O'Hara faced him squarely, poised like a bareknuckle fighter.

In a low, even voice Fergus said, "Why did you

follow me last night from the Lick House to Portsmouth Plaza?''

The question surprised Tanner: his good eye blinked several times. ''Follow you?'' he said, but the words were unconvincing as a supposedly puzzled response.

''And hurry away so quickly when I chanced to notice you.''

''You must be mistaken. I wasn't at Portsmouth Plaza last night.''

''Then it was your twin sibling, no doubt.''

Tanner looked at him in the manner of a man struggling to make a procedural decision. Then, all at once, his features smoothed and the hardness vanished; he stepped back, lifting one hand to stroke his eyepatch and then lowering it to produce a hoarhound drop from his pocket. He had redonned his mild manner, O'Hara thought with some amazement, the way a man might quickly don an article of clothing.

''Perhaps both of us are a mite too touchy about nothing whatsoever,'' Tanner said. He ate the hoarhound drop and looked at a point past O'Hara's right ear; he wore his corpse look now. ''Misunderstandings on both our parts.''

O'Hara relaxed. ''As you prefer it,'' he said.

''Fact is, I only wanted to be of help if Colfax had a problem.''

''No problem that I'm knowing of.''

Tanner nodded, paused, sucked at his candy. ''Really wasn't at Portsmouth Plaza last night, you know,'' he said, and moved past and went along the rail, aft.

O'Hara watched him turn onto the stairway there

and climb it to the weather deck. And glowered again, deeply. Perhaps Tanner *was* only a concerned friend of the gambler's, but that didn't satisfactorily explain the sudden display of anger, or why he wore a concealing mask of mildness; and it didn't explain, either, why he had baldly lied about his presence at Portsmouth Plaza. Could Tanner be the one who had stolen the gold, the one who had shot Thomas Stuart to death? But if so, why had he been so interested in Colfax—in whether or not anyone else might be involved? Or had Colfax filched the consignment after all? And, aware that he might do such as that, did Tanner expect for some reason a percentage of the booty—?

"By damn!" O'Hara muttered aloud. This business seemed to be more complicated than he had first anticipated—perhaps considerably more complicated. And with his dislike of the mysterious, that encouraged him not at all. . . .

⊷11⊷

On most packets the purser's office was located aft of the Social Hall, and that was where O'Hara found it on this one. The uniformed man who responded to his knock was the same person O'Hara had seen at the Captain's Table in the Dining Saloon earlier. Up close, he presented a rather unique appearance: tall and gaunt, with a face resembling a white raisin, and side whiskers like miniature tumbleweeds. In the middle of a long, knobbly nose was an enormous wart from which grew two thick black hairs, a half-inch or so in length hanging down on either side of the wart; the somewhat startling total effect was of a patriarchal Chinese perched atop a craggy outcropping of rock.

O'Hara forced himself not to stare at the nose. "You're Mr. Flucke?" he asked.

"I am—Titus Flucke." The purser's eyes held a somber and troubled look. "And you'd be Mr. O'Hara. The captain was here a short while ago; he told me about you."

Flucke stood aside so that O'Hara could enter and then closed the door. The office was small and almost fussily neat, containing a stand-up desk, a wall mail rack, two stools, two lighted lanterns, a stained-glass window and an overhead glass skylight, and a safe similar to but smaller than the one in the pilothouse. O'Hara seated himself on one of the stools, while Flucke sank onto the other one in front of the mail rack.

"So you know, then," O'Hara said, "about the theft of the gold shipment."

"Yes. Dreadful business." Flucke shook his head sorrowfully. "Have you made any progress in your investigation?"

"None that I'd be wanting to discuss just yet."

"I wish I could offer you some knowledge that might help, but I'm afraid I can't. I've been working here since supper. Paperwork, you know."

"You came here directly from the Dining Saloon?"

"Yes. Just as soon as the captain, Mr. Woodman, and myself parted company at the larboard rail. The captain accompanied me to the door, as a matter of fact."

"Oh, did he, now?" O'Hara said. "I had the thought he and Mr. Woodman went together from the Dining Saloon to the pilothouse."

"No, we left Mr. Woodman alone at the rail."

"And where was the captain going?"

"To his quarters."

"For what reason?"

"He didn't confide that to me."

Tugging thoughtfully at his beard, O'Hara filed this information away for further action. He said, "Do you know a gambler by the name of John A. Colfax?"

The purser made a wry mouth. "I do. He is more or less a regular passenger of ours."

"What can you tell me about him?"

"Only that I care little for him or his breed. I've long suspicioned that he's an accomplished cheat, although to my knowledge no one has ever called him down."

"You've had no trouble with him, then?"

"None to this point."

"Has he taken a stateroom this trip?"

"No," Flucke said. "Customarily he spends the entire voyage in the Gentlemen's Saloon, at one of the poker tables."

"Are you acquainted with a Mr. Charles Tanner?"

"Tanner? No, I don't believe so."

"Would you be telling me if *he* has a stateroom?"

"Of course. One moment."

Flucke drew a passenger list from a folder on the mail rack. He gave O'Hara the information: Tanner's cabin was in the texas, at the opposite end from his and Hattie's stateroom.

O'Hara stood, thanked Flucke for his cooperation, and left the office. He went straight up to the pilothouse, where he found Woodman alone at the wheel with an unlit thick black cigar protruding from one corner of his mouth. The valise and strongbox were gone from the floor, presumably shut away behind the now-closed door of the vandalized safe. The windshield was closed again, and because of the dimly lit interior and the night's darkness without, O'Hara was aware of his own faint reflection in the glass. Behind his handsome red beard, his face had the familiar

— 100 —

determination which Hattie referred to as his "trouble for everyone" expression.

"What news?" Woodman asked.

"None," O'Hara said shortly. "Have you seen the captain?"

Woodman shook his head. "Young fool Bradley was feeling dizzy from that blow on the head; the captain helped him to his quarters just after you and your wife left, and then went to make his inquiries. I warrant he's still making 'em."

"I've just spoken to Mr. Flucke," O'Hara said. He cocked a hip against the binnacle. "He said the captain and yourself parted for a time after you left the Dining Saloon tonight."

"That's right."

"The captain excused himself for his quarters?"

"He did."

"Was he explaining why?"

"No."

"What did you do after he and Mr. Flucke left you?"

"I lighted a cigar and strolled down to the main deck." Woodman gave him a wintery glare. "Look here, O'Hara, are you trying to say *I* might have had something to do with the robbery?"

"Not a bit of it," O'Hara lied.

"Then why all these questions?"

"I've to be asking all manner of questions if I'm to be getting at the truth."

Woodman grunted. "Well, I don't suppose it matters. I have nothing to hide."

O'Hara produced his pipe and put flame to the bowl. Between puffs of aromatic smoke he said, "Did you speak with anyone while you were strolling about the main deck?"

"No one."

"How long was it before you encountered the captain again?"

"I don't know. Fifteen minutes, perhaps."

Which was long enough, O'Hara thought, for either Woodman or the captain to have committed the theft, just as Colfax's fifteen-minute absence from the poker game gave the gambler opportunity. He said, "And where was it you were meeting?"

"Here on the weather deck. I had just come up the aft staircase and he had just come from his quarters."

"It was happenstance, then, that you returned here to the pilothouse together."

"Yes," Woodman said, and punctuated the word with a short, sharp blast on the pilot whistle. "Is there anything else you'd care to know, O'Hara?"

"Another fact or two, if you don't mind."

"Ask as you like, then."

"How long have you been working with young Bradley?"

"So now we've gone on to Bradley, have we? All right—about eight months."

"This wouldn't be his first position, would it?"

"His second. He was a cub on the *Antioch,* a small sternwheeler, for a year previous."

"He's had a worthy record, has he?"

"If he hadn't, I shouldn't have allowed him to work on the *Freebooty.*"

"Do you know him well?"

"As well as any man comes to know a young

— 102 —

sprout working under his care. He's a quiet lad, keeps to himself mostly; but he seems decent enough. You're wasting your time, O'Hara; I trust you're aware of that. None of this packet's officers or crew is the man we're after."

"Just as you say, Mr. Woodman."

O'Hara wandered the pilothouse, wreathing his head in great clouds of pipe smoke. Nothing came of his reflections. Woodman gave his attention to the river and to his piloting duties, reticent now; the cigar in the corner of his mouth was transformed into a shapeless, well-chewed mess.

By and by the captain returned, looking drawn and grave. "I spoke with the texas stewards and several passengers with texas staterooms," he said. "Not a soul of them noticed activity of an unusual nature tonight, or any person venturing to or from here."

Woodman said in sour tones, "O'Hara has nothing to report either—only a spate of damn-fool questions. He'll have some of the same for you in a minute, Captain."

"What sort of questions?"

"Concerning our whereabouts at the time of the robbery."

O'Hara explained his penchant for thoroughness, and the captain appeared to take this in stride. "I have no objections to telling you whatever you care to know, Mr. O'Hara."

"Well, then, you left Mr. Woodman after supper to go to your quarters—is that correct?"

"Yes."

"And you didn't see him again until you both met at the aft staircase here on the weather deck?"

"No, I did not."

"The span of time was fifteen minutes or so?"

"Thereabouts."

"Were you in your quarters the entire time?"

"I was. I had snagged a button on my coat at the supper table, and it was about to fall off; I spent the minutes repairing it with thread and needle."

O'Hara relighted his pipe. "I expect that's all I've to be inquiring about, then," he said, and added silently: For the moment.

When he left the pilothouse he went aft on the weather deck, to where the cabins of the officers and crew were located. The larger quarters had brass plates screwed to their door panels which identified them as belonging to the Captain, Chief Pilot, Purser, Chief Engineer. Of the four small cabins without identifying plates, only one, to the starboard, showed lamplight beneath the bottom of the door and through the panel louvers. O'Hara decided this was likely the one occupied by the junior pilot, Bradley, and rapped on it lightly; his judgment was proved accurate a moment later when the young blond man opened the door.

"Oh—Mr. O'Hara," Bradley said. He had wrapped a band of white cloth around his head, giving him the look of a soldier wounded in battle. But he seemed steady enough on his feet.

"How are you feeling, lad?"

"Still a bit dizzy. And my head hurts like the devil."

"I've a few more questions, if you're up to them."

"Certainly. But I don't know what more I can tell you."

Bradley pulled the cabin door wider and stepped back, allowing O'Hara to enter. The accommodation was windowless and far more spartan than the staterooms in the texas; there was a bunk along one bulkhead, a wood-and-leather bench along another, a wooden table, a small wardrobe. Draped across the bench were Bradley's gritty, grease-stained coat and baggy trousers; he had changed into clean and similarly baggy clothing.

When the junior pilot closed the door, O'Hara asked, "Now, then—you had no perception at all of the man who struck you down?"

"No, sir, none."

"Did you hear anything prior to the blow?"

"Not that I can remember."

"Dredge your memory a bit. The sound of his breathing?"

"No, sir."

"His tread?"

"Tread?"

"Light or heavy," O'Hara said. "That might be telling us if he was a big man or a small one."

Bradley started to shake his head, winced, and said, "He must have moved like a cat, Mr. O'Hara. I just don't recollect hearing any sound after the opening of the pilothouse door."

"Did you *smell* anything, perhaps? Such as sweat or pomade—a distinctive aroma?"

"No, sir, I don't think so."

"You were sitting in the pilot's seat when he hit you?"

"Yes."

"Could you tell if he did the striking from the left or right?"

"The left, I reckon," Bradley said. "The door was to my left, as you know, and I don't see any reason for him to have circled around to approach me from the right."

"There'd be a reason if he was left-handed."

"Oh. Oh, I see what you mean."

O'Hara smacked his palms together in a frustrated gesture. "Can you think of anything at all that might be helping me, lad? Even the slightest bit of a thing?"

"I only wish I could," Bradley said. "But it all happened so quickly and unexpectedly. . . . I'm sorry, Mr. O'Hara."

⊷12⊷

The table which Colfax and the others had occupied in the Gentlemen's Saloon was now empty. The gambler was not among the crowd of men in the room, nor was Tanner or the miner or even Horace T. Goatleg. O'Hara went out into the Social Hall, and there he spied the newspaperman helping himself to cold cuts at the refreshment tables.

He sauntered over and stood in next to the reporter, who nodded and gave him a companionable smile. "Have Colfax and yourself given up on the Saloon for the evening?" O'Hara asked.

"As far as drinking goes, yes." A rueful smile. "I'll not want a head tomorrow as large as today's. But I imagine the poker game will continue when he returns from his ten o'clock engagement. As great as his luck has been tonight, a poker table is nothing less than a field white for the sickle."

O'Hara said, "Engagement, did you say?"

"With a lady—or perhaps not such a lady." The newspaperman chuckled softly. "Those are Colfax's words, not mine."

"Did he happen to be mentioning the lady's name?"

"Not in my hearing. You seem rather absorbed in Colfax's activities, if you don't mind my saying so."

"It's my wife's cousin, you see," O'Hara said, putting a trace of worried indignation into his voice. "She's a precocious one and easily swayed by a glib tongue. My wife noticed her conversing with Colfax before we departed San Francisco and is a mite fearful for the girl's virtue. She's asked me to keep an eye on matters."

The reporter nodded, serious now. "Perhaps Colfax's engagement was with some other young lady entirely."

"Aye, I hope so."

O'Hara speared a slice of ham, bade the newspaperman good night, and drifted out of the Hall. He was rather pleased with his lie, which had only in that moment occurred to him, and he thought that he would use it again when next he spoke with Tanner; it might help him smooth over the earlier incident and thereby allow him to do a bit of subtle probing without further arousing the one-eyed man.

On the weather deck again, he entered the tunnel down the center of the texas and stopped before the door to Tanner's stateroom, Number 14. No light showed within, and when O'Hara knocked there was no response.

As he turned away and started forward, Hattie appeared at the tunnel entrance in that direction. She saw him, gestured animatedly, and hurried up to him. "I've been looking all over for you, Fergus," she said. "I've discovered a fact or two that may or may not have meaning, but I find them interesting, in any case."

"What fact or two, my lady?"

"We had best go inside our cabin first, where it's private."

He shrugged slightly and unlocked the door to their stateroom. Hattie said as he lighted one of the lamps, "I decided after you left me that if your mind was made up to involve us in this gold thievery business, I might as well embark on a little investigating of my own. I'm not partial to being left out of things, you know." She fixed him with a steady eye. "And from the looks of you, you haven't investigated up much yourself."

"You mentioned a fact or two," O'Hara reminded her grumpily.

"Well, did you know, first of all, that the captain and Mr. Woodman did not come directly from the Dining Saloon to the pilothouse, as we might have assumed?"

"I did. The purser informed me of it. Woodman claims to have been walking about on the main deck and the captain to have gone to his quarters to repair a snagged button on his coat."

Hattie's eyes grew bright. "Mr. Woodman may be telling the truth," she said, "but the captain isn't."

"How d'you know that?"

"In the Ladies' Cabin I spoke with a certain Mrs. Yount from Stockton, who happened to see the captain entering one of the staterooms here on the texas shortly after supper. She remembers the time because she had left the Dining Saloon at the same time as he, only a few minutes before. He was acting a bit surreptitious, Mrs. Yount claims—and he was carrying a small bundle."

O'Hara's interest was keen now. "Which stateroom was this?"

"She wasn't certain of the number."

"But she was certain that it was the captain?"

"One could hardly mistake the man in his uniform."

"Aye," he agreed. "What could Mrs. Yount tell you of the bundle?"

"Only that it was small and appeared heavy," Hattie said. "She had but a glimpse of it."

O'Hara circled the cabin three times, like a dog about to lie down. But he had no intention of resting; on the contrary, the more he considered it, it seemed to him that the time had come for positive and direct action. What that action should be became clear to him on the third circuit of the room.

"Wait here, my lady," he said decisively. "I'll be back in quick time."

"Where are you going?"

"I'll explain when I return. Five minutes."

Hattie started to say something else, but O'Hara was already on his way out, hurrying. He went straight to the purser's office, found Titus Flucke still there, and requested a copy of the passenger list for the twenty staterooms in the texas. Flucke obliged. When O'Hara emerged three minutes later, he had not only the copy in his possession but a set of master keys as well, which he had dexterously appropriated from the pegboard on the office wall. He had not asked Flucke for the keys because he wanted no one except Hattie to know what he planned to do, least of all one of the

Freebooty's officers, and because it was doubtful the purser would have consented to the loan no matter what manner of excuse was presented to him. Flucke might eventually realize the master set was missing, but O'Hara would cross that bridge if and when he came to it.

The moment he reentered their stateroom, Hattie demanded, "Now just where did you rush off to?"

O'Hara told her, and showed her the set of keys.

"The purser gave those to you, did he?"

"Well, not precisely."

"Which means, I gather, that you filched them."

"There was nothing else to be done, in the circumstances."

"What you're planning is a search of the captain's quarters, isn't it?"

"It is."

"And if the gold isn't there?"

"Then I'll be searching the cabins of the other crew members, just to be certain, and as many other accommodations here in the texas as I can be getting into."

"Have you gone daft? You can't expect to enter a score of staterooms without being caught eventually—"

"You'll be there to see that I'm not."

"—and that can only mean more trouble. I—" She stopped abruptly. "I'll be what?"

"You'll be there to see that I'm not," O'Hara said. "I'll be needing you to act as lookout."

"Fergus, this is a *ridiculous* scheme. The gold could be hidden in a hundred other places on board this steamer, and you want us to—"

"I've conducted myself in the approved detective

fashion the past two hours," O'Hara said stubbornly, "and I've learned not a confounded whit. It's time to be taking drastic measures if I'm to be producing the proper results. Now then, will you be helping me, or would you prefer I set about my task alone and unaided?"

Hattie sighed. "I expect I had better," she said, "if only to keep you from getting your mulish head bashed in. Sometimes I wonder why I consented to marry you."

"Because you loved me and couldn't resist my clever advances."

She blushed faintly. "Partly that, and partly because I knew that if I said no, you'd have hounded me till Judgment Day. You're the most obstinate man on the face of this good earth."

"I take that as a compliment," O'Hara said, and hurried her out and down the central corridor.

When they came out to the aft section of the texas, the area there was empty of passengers and stewards. All the cabins belonging to the *Freebooty*'s officers and crew, including Bradley's, were darkened. Except for the pulsing cadence of the buckets, the steady *Ssoo, hah!* of the piston in counterpoint, it was very still.

O'Hara stepped up to the door marked CAPTAIN, listened, heard nothing, nodded to himself, and came back to Hattie. Moonshine and shadow made a plaid design on the deck boarding, and he took her into one of the ebon patches.

"You situate yourself hereabouts," he whispered. "If the captain should happen along, fetch up a pretext of some sort to take him safely away."

"Suppose someone else should happen by?"

"What you do then is hum a bit of 'The Union Forever,' loud enough so I can be hearing you. I'll be searching by matchlight, and if you commence humming I'll douse the flame and stand fast until you stop again."

Hattie nodded dubiously and moved over toward the hogging beam, around the texas corner from which was the aft stairway.

O'Hara checked the texas tunnel, saw that it was still deserted, and approached the captain's door again. He tried three of the master keys before he found the one that turned the latchbolt; then he slipped quickly inside and closed the door after him.

The curtains were open on the single starboard window, and a shaft of moonlight offered enough illumination for him to make out the shapes of the furnishings. He paused, heard nothing from without. He struck a match on his thumbnail and proceeded, first, to a large trunk at the foot of the single bunkbed. The trunk was not locked; he raised the iron-banded lid.

The heat of the match flame became uncomfortable, and O'Hara shook it out, blew on the burned sliver of wood and then carefully put it into his coat pocket. He struck another match and began to sift through the contents of the trunk: clothing, a stack of issues of *The California Police Gazette*, a Beadle dime novel called *Seth Jones, or The Captives of the Frontier* which looked interesting but which O'Hara had no present inclination to appropriate for himself, and a variety of mementoes that included a woman's perfumed garter. But that was all.

He searched the cabin wardrobe, examined the

area under the bunkbed, and rummaged through the drawers in the rolltop desk affixed to the forward bulkhead. Then he entered the captain's private toilet. When he emerged again seconds later he was satisfied, unhappily so, that the consignment of gold dust was nowhere in these premises.

He slipped out as quickly as he had entered and relocked the door. Hattie approached him from larboard. "Nothing, I see," she said dryly.

O'Hara gave a curt nod. "I'll be taking the chief pilot's cabin next," he told her, and went to the door to Woodman's quarters.

That cabin, however, also yielded negative results. And so, subsequently, did the purser's accommodations. He knocked softly on Bradley's door before using the master key, in the event the junior pilot had retired early because of his head wound; but there was no answer—Bradley might perhaps have gone back to the pilothouse—and when he entered cautiously he confirmed that the cabin was unoccupied.

O'Hara had just opened the wardrobe when he heard Hattie abruptly begin humming "The Union Forever." He blew out his match and padded back to the door. Thirty seconds passed, without incident or audible exchange of words, and then the humming ceased. A strolling passenger, he decided, or someone with a texas stateroom. He resumed his search, but there was nothing, it developed, for him to find there either.

He was beginning to feel irritable. He had commenced this plan of action with at least a modest expectation of success, and thus far it had provided him with the same lack of positive information as had his more proper investigative techniques. Still, he was not yet ready to abandon the searching procedure; there were still the texas staterooms to be looked at.

When he emerged from Bradley's cabin, Hattie said, "I signaled you because a man and his wife came around the corner from the stairway. My Lord, I jumped a foot when I saw them. And I can imagine what they thought of me when I began humming like a foolish minstrel."

"You're doing fine, my lady," O'Hara said abstractedly.

"Fergus, will you please give up this skulking about?"

"Mr. Charles Tanner's next on my list," he said. "I'd like to be knowing a bit more about that lad anyway, even if I shouldn't be turning up the gold in his stateroom. He's not the mild, self-effacing gent he appears to be, you know."

Hattie lifted her hands, palms up, then dropped them again defeatedly. She didn't resist when O'Hara guided her into the empty texas tunnel and along it to the door to Number 14.

As before, only darkness showed through the louvers and below the sill. O'Hara eased the key into the latch, gesturing to Hattie with to and fro motions that he wanted her to move about the tunnel rather than stand in one spot. She folded her arms across her bosom and walked a few paces forward, watching him over her shoulder.

O'Hara released the bolt, entered Tanner's stateroom, and immediately closed the door behind him. The curtains were partially drawn over the larboard window, which was open by several inches; a faint shaft of light and the cool, moist smell of the river penetrated the cabin. He withdrew a match from the dwindling supply in his coat pocket—

And something made a noise in front of him.

He pulled back against the door, listening. The noise came again, an odd sort of fluttering—and then there was a low-pitched and inhuman moan that sent an involuntary shiver rippling along O'Hara's spine. A diminishing series of maniacal cackles followed.

A voice said, "Goddamn your heathen eyes."

O'Hara snapped the match into flame, his mouth turning wolfish. The first thing he saw in the phosphorous glare was the center table, and on it, raising one claw as though to shut out the sudden light, was the miner's huge parrot. The bird squawked in protest, backed away, nearly fell off the table, said, "Horse dung," and flapped upward and backward to settle on top of the wardrobe.

The table and the antics of the parrot were not all that O'Hara saw in the match flare: he saw also the figure of a man sprawled supine on one of the two bunks.

He stood rigid, and the first thought that crossed his mind was that Tanner had returned to the cabin and gone to bed. But the man on the bunk had appeared to be fully clothed. There was no sound of stirring, as there should have been by now, and finally O'Hara came forward with the match held out in front of him. When he reached the bunk he leaned down for a closer inspection.

The short hairs rose on the back of his neck. Charles Tanner was not sleeping, except in the Biblical sense of "eternal rest." He had been stabbed several times in the chest; the fronts of his shirt and sack coat were saturated with blood.

With perfect solemnity and surprising accuracy, the parrot said, "Deader than a hobnail, boys."

⊰13⊱

O'Hara lit one of the lamps; there was little reason now for matchlight alone. The center table was littered with hoarhound drops and the remnants of a paper candy sack—which, coupled with the partly open window, gave one possible explanation for the parrot's presence. The bird glared down at him from the wardrobe in a malevolently challenging way.

"Men can too," it said. "Take no chances."

"Aye," O'Hara muttered. "And where's your master, you bundle of painted feathers? Gone to clean off the stains of murder, perhaps?"

"Night sign, night sign," the parrot said. Then it said, "Hump me for a swaybacked mule," and flew down to the window, made its flatulent noise, cackled hysterically, and disappeared into the night outside.

Scowling, O'Hara turned toward the bunk on which the body lay. Tanner wore his corpse look—and because now it was genuine, it seemed even more ludicrous. Fergus stepped closer, and for the first time he noticed that the eyepatch had been pulled askew.

The amazing thing about this was that the one-eyed man had not been a one-eyed man at all. In fact there did not seem to be anything at all wrong with the eye beneath the patch: the eyeball was intact and stared in exactly the same presently sightless but un-clouded manner as its twin.

Now why, O'Hara thought bemusedly, would a man wear an eyepatch if he had no need for one?

Tanner's bloody coat had been laid aside and folded back, and when O'Hara slid careful fingers into the inside pocket he found it empty. The same was true of both outer pockets. He turned the body enough to feel all the trouser pockets and determine that those too were devoid of contents.

The motive for Tanner's murder could be rob-bery, then—merely a coincidence on the heels of Stuart's death in San Francisco and the theft of the gold shipment. O'Hara, however, did not believe that for an instant. The stabbing of Tanner was somehow related to those other two crimes: he no longer held any reservations about the interrelationship of what had happened in San Francisco and what was taking place on board the *Freebooty*.

The blood on Tanner's chest had dried to a thick reddish-brown, which meant he had been dead for some time—perhaps, O'Hara thought, since not long after he had spoken to him on the deckhouse. Had Tanner gone from there to confront Colfax, or possibly a nameless third person in whom he had implied in-terest, and subsequently been killed for his efforts? And had he been murdered because, as was probable in the case of Stuart, his accomplice or accomplices wanted either to silence him or to eliminate his share in the booty? Or was it possible that Tanner had not been directly involved in the robbery, but had suspected the truth, had approached the culprits for the purpose of hijack or blackmail, and been given the knife for that reason?

O'Hara peered at the bunk. The bed linen was neatly turned down, doubtless by one of the texas stewards, and there was no sign of blood on it. That fact appeared to indicate that Tanner had been killed elsewhere and then transported here. Assuming this was so, the scene of the murder had to be propinquitous to this stateroom—certainly somewhere on the weather deck; it was hardly likely that the murderer could have carried the body, as bloody as it was, from one of the lower decks without running the enormous risk of discovery.

The obvious reason for such transportation was that the deed had been done in the cabin or stateroom of the assassin. Putting the body in Tanner's own accommodation would therefore accomplish two objectives: it would remove the damning presence of a corpse, and, under ordinary circumstances, it would keep the murder itself a secret until after the *Freebooty* docked at Stockton in the morning.

O'Hara pondered. Did the miner who owned the parrot have a texas stateroom? It didn't seem likely, considering the manner in which the man had been dressed and his general demeanor—but the bird's presence here in Tanner's stateroom, and the miner's acquaintance with Tanner and Colfax, nevertheless now firmly placed him on the list of suspects. It was not a certainty, after all, that Tanner had been stabbed in another cabin or stateroom; he could have met his fate swiftly in some darkened area of the weather deck, such as aft by the hogging beam, and then been carried here. Colfax, as well, could not be eliminated from the list for this very reason. . . .

O'Hara cursed eloquently under his breath. This entire affair was not merely complicated, and growing even more complicated at every new turn; it was becoming a damned torture box for the devilment of Fergus O'Hara—one in which he ran from here to there, suffered exquisite anguish—and solved nothing.

Nevertheless, "giving up" was not a phrase to be found in his lexicon; and furthermore, he had faith that St. Patrick intended to see him through if only he would persevere. So he commenced a search of the stateroom, starting with a small carpetbag that sat on one of the chairs, catches unfastened. The contents had been riffled, it seemed, since they were in a state of disarray. Now what had the murderer been looking for among Tanner's belongings? The gold? Evidence pointing to his identity? Whatever it was, he had apparently found it, or it had not been there in the first place; O'Hara discovered nothing among the clothing and toilet articles that told him anything of a helpful nature.

He crossed to the wardrobe just as, from out in the tunnel, Hattie burst into an urgent humming of "The Union Forever."

O'Hara went to the bulkhead lamp and extinguished the flame. He felt his way silently to the door, heard heavy footsteps approaching from forward and lighter ones from aft. Both stopped almost directly opposite the door, and the jovial voice of Horace Goatleg said, "Ah, Mrs. O'Hara, good evening. You sound in a sprightly mood."

Hattie ceased humming. When she said, "I feel so, Mr. Goatleg; it's a lovely evening," she sounded embarrassed.

"Indeed it is. Have you been out for a walk?"

"Yes. With my husband."

"Is Mr. O'Hara still out on deck?"

"I believe he's gone to the Saloon."

"Well, perhaps I'll encounter him there," Goatleg said, and murmured a parting good night.

Hattie began humming again as the fat man's steps receded along the tunnel; seconds later she lapsed into silence to let O'Hara know that the tunnel was once more free.

He stood for a moment by the door, frowning. He had more or less forgotten Goatleg; but now he recalled having seen his name on the passenger list—the fat man also had a texas stateroom. Goatleg seemed deeply involved with Tanner and Colfax—O'Hara himself had last night thought what a strange three-some they made—and the nature of his relationship with the dead man was not at all clear. Another good suspect. But, confound it, why couldn't he narrow the list *down* instead of continually widening it with likely new prospects?

Striking a match, he came away from the door and continued his search of the stateroom. The wardrobe was empty, as was the remainder of the cabin—just as he had expected. He returned to the door, heard only stillness without, and opened it and stepped into the tunnel. He did not bother to relatch the bolt.

He saw Hattie standing near their own stateroom forward, gestured to her to remain where she was. Then he crossed to Number 8, Goatleg's cabin. Once inside, he went through the now-familiar exploration procedure in rapid time. In one of Goat-leg's two pieces of luggage he found several papers. He took a moment to glance through them, saw that they all pertained to land development business in Northern California. Otherwise, he found nothing at all.

When he slipped out this time, he almost bumped into Hattie. She looked determined now. "Before you enter any more staterooms or do anything else, Fergus O'Hara, I want words with you in the privacy of our cabin."

O'Hara hesitated; then, because he was not yet sure of his next step anyway, he nodded.

And across from them the door to Number 9 opened abruptly and the gambler, Colfax, appeared.

When he saw Hattie and O'Hara he stopped in mid-stride, startled—but only for a second. He had a freshly washed and toileted appearance; his hair was damp, and he smelled, O'Hara thought, not unlike a bouquet of pansies, the result of a liberal dousing with lavender water. He also had the appearance of a fox leaving a henhouse, which is to say he seemed quite pleased with himself.

O'Hara said with underplayed interest, "I didn't know you had a stateroom here in the texas, Mr. Colfax. It seems you told me earlier that you hadn't been up on the weather deck at all this trip."

Colfax shrugged. "This isn't my stateroom," he said. "I've been—ah—visiting with a friend."

"A pleasant visit, I trust."

"Most pleasant," Colfax said. He gaze held O'Hara's for half a dozen seconds, then dropped away. "If you'll excuse me . . ."

He bowed and moved past them, walking in long

strides. O'Hara watched him leave the tunnel and disappear to larboard, then removed the passenger list from his pocket and scanned the arrangement of names. Number 9, it developed, belonged to a Miss Annabelle Thatch of San Francisco.

Hattie tugged at his arm, and O'Hara went with her to their stateroom. When they were inside and the door was safely closed, she said, "Now what was that little exchange with Mr. Colfax about?"

O'Hara said, "A matter of illicit trifling, I expect."

"What?"

"Colfax's friend is a lady by the name of Annabelle Thatch."

"Oh, I see," Hattie said disapprovingly. She sat down on her bunk. "Fergus, what did you find in Charles Tanner's stateroom?"

He frowned. "What makes you think I found anything at all?"

"The length of time you were in there, your lighting of the lamp, the odd squawking speech of a parrot, the expression on your face when you came out, and the fact that you didn't lock the door again, as you did on all the other cabins."

O'Hara looked at her admiringly. "You're a fair good detective yourself, my lady."

"Answer my question," Hattie said.

He had not wanted to tell her of Tanner's murder; a second homicide, this one on board the steamer, would only serve to set her fretting and deepen her conviction that their involvement in the whole affair was both unnecessary and precarious. But now that she knew he had found something in the stateroom, he did not doubt that she would slip down there and enter it herself if he refused to confide in her.

"All right," he said. "But before I tell you, you're to understand that I won't be listening to any more arguments about discontinuing my investigation. I'm certain now that Stuart's murder and the gold theft are connected, and the settling of personal accounts is more than sufficient reason for me to fetch out the truth. It's as much a matter of pride as anything else."

"No further arguments," Hattie said. "I've resigned myself to the situation—as I've had to do a dozen times before."

O'Hara explained about the murder of Charles Tanner, the presence of the parrot, the fact that Tanner's eyepatch had evidently concealed a perfectly good eye. She didn't interrupt. As a reward he went on to tell her of his suspicions of Colfax, his encounter with Tanner, and his questioning of Flucke, Woodman, the captain, and Bradley.

Hattie worried her lower lip speculatively. "If Tanner *was* murdered in someone else's stateroom," she said, "do you think it could have been Miss Annabelle Thatch's? Which would make Colfax the cutthroat, of course."

"A possibility," O'Hara agreed. "I'll pay a call on her shortly to see what can be learned."

"I wonder if it also could have been her stateroom that the captain entered after supper. Any female who would consent to trifling with that gambler is suspect of any number of sins. You don't suppose she's a harlot, do you?"

He grinned. "I'll let you know after I've spent some time in her company."

Hattie made a rude noise. "The captain might also have entered *Tanner's* stateroom, mightn't he?"

"Aye. He's another I've to be having a talk with shortly."

"Do you intend to tell him you're aware of the murder?"

"I do. If he's innocent, he's a right to know. If he's not, the shock of a blunt revelation might bring forth a guilty slip."

Hattie said, "Who else will you be seeing?"

"The miner, I expect."

"Perhaps you should question the parrot, too."

O'Hara was not amused. "Bah," he said.

"You don't plan to search any more staterooms, I hope."

"Not unless all else fails. I'm no longer as taken with the idea as I was in the beginning—although you've to be admitting it did yield Tanner's corpse."

"Some yield." Hattie was silent for a moment; then she stood up. "Fergus. I think I ought to accompany you on these rounds you intend to make."

"For what reason?"

"You might need me, if only for safety's sake."

"Safety's sake?"

"You're after a man who has already twice committed murder," she said. "Such a man wouldn't hesitate to kill a third time if he found it necessary, and what more likely prospect than you?"

"You're assuming he knows of my investigation."

"As well he may."

O'Hara snorted. He had already considered this possibility and decided that it wasn't worth concerning himself about; in fact, he would rather welcome it, if it was the only way his man could be unmasked and the mystery solved. "Hattie," he said, "the sun hasn't yet dawned on the day I'm unable to be taking care of my own self."

"If I were along, he wouldn't dare come after you."

"How d'you know he wouldn't? You can't tell what a desperate man will do. No, I'll not be placing you in danger, or using you to circumvent it, either. Besides that, I've another task for you to undertake."

"What task?"

"Hie down to the Ladies' Cabin and see if you can relocate the woman who told you about the captain—Mrs. Yount. Question her a bit more, if you do find her, and see if you can't joggle her memory as to which stateroom he entered, or at least to give you a better idea of which one. Come find me directly, should you gain any positive results. Otherwise, you might see what you can find out about Miss Annabelle Thatch and her relationship with Colfax."

That appeared to capture Hattie's fancy. "I could also ask about certain others, such as your Mr. Goatleg."

"Why him in particular?"

"I don't like him any more than Colfax."

"And why not?"

"He reminds me of that man in Cheyenne—Cobb."

The individual to whom she referred was a self-proclaimed promoter and the author of a scheme, among other venal endeavors, for selling rancid foodstuffs to reservation Indians in Wyoming Territory; he had been severely dealt with by O'Hara the previous year. "You shouldn't judge Goatleg because he's fat and jovial and calls to mind a scoundrel like Cobb."

"Perhaps not," Hattie said, but in a voice that said she hadn't changed her mind any. "Well and good, then; I'll go the Ladies' Cabin. But I'll take your promise to be watchful first."

O'Hara gave it, and they left the stateroom and went out of the texas to the forward stairway. When Hattie had started down, he paused for a moment to ponder. The captain first, or the miner, or Miss Annabelle Thatch? He made his choice, predicated on the adage of "striking while the iron is still hot." Then, smiling somewhat wickedly at the vulgar pun implied in that, he reentered the texas and knocked with authority on the door panel of Number 9.

~14~

The girl who opened the door was in her early twenties—large-boned, large-bosomed, with childishly ingenuous features and an air of infatuation. Short flaxen curls, slightly disarrayed at the moment, fringed the roundness of her face, and her cheeks were flushed; enormous brown eyes sparkled in much the same way Hattie's had yesterday, after the hour in the Lick House's fine four-poster. She wore a green balmoral skirt, a basque waist, and an embroidered sack coat.

Tiny parallel ridges appeared on her forehead as she gazed at O'Hara. "Yes?"

"Miss Thatch?"

She nodded. "I don't believe I've made your acquaintance, have I?"

"I expect not," O'Hara said. He hadn't known exactly how he would go about eliciting information from Annabelle Thatch, but now that he had seen her, he decided that a direct and authoritative approach would be best. "My name is O'Hara, Fergus O'Hara. It happens I'm an operative of the Pinkerton Police, Chicago."

Miss Thatch's eyes and mouth widened. "Police?" she said, bewildered. "Why . . . what on earth would a *policeman* want with me?"

"I've a few questions to be asking, if you don't mind."

"Questions?"

"Concerning Mr. John A. Colfax."

"Mr. Colfax?" The flush on her cheeks deepened. "But he couldn't *possibly* have done anything . . . disreputable?"

O'Hara had never been fond of individuals of either sex who constantly expressed themselves in the interrogative, as seemed to be the case with Miss Thatch. He narrowed his eyes sternly. "It would be best if we conversed within," he said.

"Oh, well, I . . . well, if you feel it's necessary?"

"I do."

Flustered, she backed away inside. O'Hara entered, latched the door, and looked about the stateroom. The linen on one of the bunkbeds was disheveled, rather violently so, but nothing else was out of place or out of the ordinary; a bandbox and a reticule sat on the floor inside the open wardrobe.

"Why do you want to ask questions about John—Mr. Colfax? He *hasn't* done anything, has he?"

O'Hara asked, "How long have you known the man, Miss Thatch?"

"I met him in San Francisco two weeks ago," she answered, making a statement at last. "But—"

"D'you yourself live in San Francisco?"

"Yes, I'm a care worker at St. Patrick's Orphan Asylum?"

Looking at her closely, O'Hara decided she was telling the truth about that. He felt a bit more favorably disposed toward her; despite her apparent flaws in character, she was engaged in a worthy profession—and one that functioned under the benevolent name of the patron saint of Ireland, to boot.

He said, "Have you family in Stockton?"

"I've no family anywhere. I was raised by the people of St. Patrick's?"

"Then you're making this trip for what reason?"

She flushed again. "I've some time off, and I thought it might be pleasant to experience a steamer voyage . . . ?"

Meaning, O'Hara thought, that she had booked passage on the *Freebooty* in order to have a comfortable place in which she and Colfax could trifle. He said, "You entertained Colfax for a time this evening, didn't you, Miss Thatch?"

Flame-red color suffused her entire face now, and she glanced guiltily at the rumpled bedding. "I . . . well, he stopped by for a few moments . . ."

"Was it at ten o'clock that he arrived?"

"Precisely at ten, yes."

"Did anyone else come calling while he was here?"

"Anyone else? Oh, no; we . . . we were quite alone."

"Was he stepping out himself for any length of time?"

"No. We—um—we . . ." She trailed off into silence.

"Did you entertain any other visitors this evening?"

"Certainly not," she said, offended.

"Were you here between eight and nine?"

"No, I was in the Ladies' Cabin?"

"Then you didn't see the captain during that hour?"

"The captain? Of the packet?"

"The same."

"I can't recall that I've *ever* seen him. Mr. O'Hara—"

He put up a staying hand. "Tell me this: did Colfax give you something to be keeping for him? Such as a grip or a bandbox or any other container?"

She shook her head; her bewilderment seemed even greater.

"That bandbox yonder in the wardrobe is yours?"

"It is, yes."

"Would you mind if I looked at the contents?"

"But . . . why? What are you trying to find?"

"Certain property," O'Hara said vaguely. "You can open the bandbox yourself, and I'll not be touching anything of your personal belongings."

She hesitated, then shrugged in a nervously confused way and led him to the wardrobe. There was nothing inside the bandbox, however, except for clothing and other feminine articles, none of which were of expensive manufacture. Without being asked, she also opened the reticule. The gold was obviously not there either; the only interesting item it contained—interesting because O'Hara did not know why she should have it, though perhaps in this case ignorance was bliss—was a brown bottle of patent medicine labeled *GONO, Man's Friend for Gonor-*

rhoea and Gleet. An unequaled remedy for all un-
natural discharges. Allays inflammation and cures
gonorrhoea and gleet. Will not cause stricture.

O'Hara turned away and inspected the remainder
of the stateroom. He saw no place else where the gold
might be secreted. Looking again at the girl, he asked,
"What d'you know of Colfax, Miss Thatch?"

Some of the sparkle returned to her eyes. "Oh,
that he's sweet and intelligent and . . . gentle? I've
never met a man like him before; he's so, well,
worldly?"

No doubt, O'Hara thought sourly. He said,
"What did he tell you was his profession?"

"He has been quite honest about the fact that he's
a gambler," Miss Thatch said. "I can't imagine there
is anything wrong with that, so long as it's honest
gambling?"

He ruminated silently for a moment. As far as he
could tell, Miss Annabelle Thatch had been more or
less frank with him, and it did not seem probable that
she was a party to the likes of thievery and murder.
Nor was it probable that she was the person the captain had visited after supper. Colfax, however, was
still very definitely a suspect. O'Hara calculated that it
had been approximately half past nine when he had
encountered Charles Tanner outside the Social Hall;
and the newspaperman had told him that Colfax had
closed up his poker game shortly thereafter, which
was sufficient time for the gambler to have encountered Tanner, stabbed him, taken the body to Tanner's
stateroom, searched the premises, and then come to
keep his ten o'clock rendezvous with Miss Thatch.

The issue of the moment, therefore, was what he

should be telling this foolish young lady on the matter of Colfax. He did not like the gambler, and there was little doubt that Colfax had any but dishonorable intentions toward her, even if he should be innocent of murder and other crimes; the way he had so impertinently looked at Hattie this afternoon, and the reporter's account of his callous remarks concerning his engagement with Miss Thatch, bore out this opinion.

So, trusting his instincts, he said, "The fact of the matter is, I've reason to believe Colfax is a sharper and a womanizer—and perhaps even worse than that. I've been on his trail for some little time now in connection with certain unlawful activities."

Miss Thatch said, "Womanizer?" as if that were the most terrible word in the English language, and put a hand to her mouth. Her eyes lost all remnants of their earlier sparkle.

"You understand," O'Hara told her gently, "you'd do well not to become any more involved with him than you already are. It can only lead you to grief."

"But he said he . . . and I allowed him to . . ." She looked at O'Hara in a tragic way. "Are you *certain* he's what you say he is?"

"Aye, I'm certain."

"Oh!" she said, and went to one of the beds—not the disheveled one—and sank onto it. She sat there stiffly, hands fisted in her lap. O'Hara thought she was about to cry; he shifted uncomfortably on his feet and started to say something inadequate about her being young and strong and able to survive such disillusionments. But before he could get the words out, he saw her eyes begin to harden until they were like brown agates.

And she said, "Why, that son of a mongrel bitch."

O'Hara blinked.

"That fancy-dressed, sweet-talking, fornicating horse's ass."

O'Hara blinked again.

"That handsome, lecherous, bastard father of a whoremonger," Miss Thatch said. "That—that—"

"I expect you've summed it up well enough, now," O'Hara said mildly, although he was rather impressed by her abrupt display of spirit, not to mention the inventiveness and vehemence of her language.

Miss Thatch looked at him blankly for a moment. Then she said, with no hint of embarrassment, "If I were a man, I believe I would find a pistol and shoot Mr. John A. Colfax squarely in his manhood. I'd have every right, wouldn't I?"

"It's best if you do nothing at all," O'Hara told her hurriedly. He did not think that even the likes of Colfax should be shot in the manhood by an irate woman. "I'll be seeing to Colfax's fate myself, perhaps—or there'll be others later on who will. You've not to be confronting him, Miss Thatch; and you've not to be telling him under any circumstances of my visit or of the conversation we've had."

"I never want to see him again," Miss Thatch said.

"That's a wise decision, if you'll stand by it."

"Oh, I will. As soon as we arrive in Stockton, I'll make immediate arrangements to return to San Francisco. In fact, I have just decided definitely to go through with the wedding."

"Wedding?"

"To James Fuller, my beau? It's all organized for next week? At least *he* truly loves me—and he should be all cured by now."

Which told O'Hara what she was doing with the bottle of GONO (he still thought ignorance had been bliss), and also told him that he had worried for naught over Miss Thatch. His sympathies, for that matter, now lay more with James Fuller, cured or not.

He murmured a parting, left her to ponder her sins past and present, and went forward to the pilothouse. Woodman was there at the wheel, and Bradley beside him, but the captain was nowhere to be seen. O'Hara asked where he might be.

"Gone down to the engine room," Woodman said. "Minor trouble with one of the feed pumps."

O'Hara saw no purpose in telling the two pilots of Tanner's murder—at least not until after he had talked with the captain. He answered with vagaries their questions on the progress of his investigation, and walked out as abruptly as he had entered.

Few passengers were abroad on the deckhouse, it now being somewhat past midnight. Most of those with main-deck steerage, he saw when he came down the second forward stairway, were rolled into blankets in wagons or among personal belongings, or else gathered in small groups for quiet conversation. He neither saw nor heard the Mulrooney Guards, and wondered perfunctorily if they had all drained their jugs of poteen and fallen into peaceful slumber.

The night air had developed a chill, and there

were ragged layers of mist, like yards upon yards of tattered lace, among the tule reeds in one of the sloughs the *Freebooty* was currently passing. O'Hara tugged up the collar on his sack coat as he hurried aft through faint pools of lantern light and deep cargo-cast shadows.

When he entered the engine room, however, he not only lowered his collar but opened his coat and loosened his cravat. Lighted by big square brass bulkhead-lanterns, the room was filled with thick heat, the rumbling sound of the furnace fires, and the sharp pungency of warm cylinder oil; it was also filled with a maze of machinery: the boilers, piping columns, gauges, feed pumps, air pumps, pumps for fire and bilges and sanitary systems, and the massive apparatus of the walking-beam engine. Consisting of cylinder, valve-gear, beam and crank, the walking-beam was slung in trunnions at the top of the A-shaped gallows frame which projected above the weather deck; with each stroke of the huge piston, a roar of steam escaped through the exhaust valve.

There were five men presently in the enclosure, including the captain, who was conversing with a bear-sized man in greasy denims, likely the chief engineer. An assistant or "striker" was busy with the burnished-steel wheel of the condenser valve, and two muscled, sweating Negro firemen continually fed four-foot lengths of bull-pine into the blazing furnaces. Deckhands would move in and out at regular intervals, bringing trundles of fresh wood from the stacked cords outside.

The engineer scowled as O'Hara approached. "Hell and damnation," he said irritably, "can't you read posted signs? Passengers are forbidden on these premises—"

"It's all right, Gores," the captain said. He gave O'Hara an anxious look. "News of moment?"

"Cheerless moment. Could we be speaking in private, Captain?"

The captain nodded, and they left the engine room and made their way to a deserted area near the taffrail. "What have you discovered, Mr. O'Hara?" the packet master asked.

O'Hara rebuttoned his coat. "First off," he said flatly, "I've discovered that you told me a lie earlier."

"Here, what do you mean by that?"

"You said you went directly to your quarters after supper, when you left Woodman and the purser. I've reliable information that you entered one of the staterooms in the texas, carrying a bundle of some sort. D'you deny that?"

The captain's face had registered emotion, but in the darkness O'Hara could not be certain of what it was. In any case, the captain did not lose his composure. He said, tight-lipped, "Whether I did or did not enter a texas stateroom after supper is none of your concern. It has nothing to do with the issue of the gold theft."

"That remains to be determined, in light of recent developments."

"What recent developments?"

"A murder, in one of the texas staterooms."

"What?" The captain sounded genuinely shocked—but again, he did not lose his composure. "My God, who was killed?"

"A man named Charles Tanner."

"I don't recognize the name. Are you positive it was murder?"

"He was stabbed several times in the chest."

"Good Christ," the captain said. He leaned on the rail in a stunned way. "You think his death is connected with the theft?"

"I do."

"Have you evidence of it?"

"None but my own intuition."

"Well, are there any suspects?"

"A riverboat full of them, passengers and officers."

The captain bristled this time. "Meaning me, I expect. I resent your implication, O'Hara. If I entered a texas stateroom tonight, it was not that of a man named Charles Tanner."

"Which was it, then?"

"Look here, O'Hara, I am the master of this packet, and it is only through my good offices that you've been allowed to investigate what has happened. I'll not be subjected to undue harassment from you. I am guilty of no crime, and my private affairs are just that: private."

O'Hara shrugged elaborately. "As you wish, Captain."

"I have a question for you, come to think of it." The captain was still nettled. "How did you happen to find this man Tanner, if his body is in his stateroom?"

"I fancied a word or two with the lad," O'Hara said glibly, "and I noted his latch wasn't secured when I arrived. I considered this curious, so I poked my head inside. It was in the lantern light from the tunnel that I saw him sprawled out on one of the bunks."

The captain appeared to find this satisfactory. "I warrant I'd best have a look for myself."

O'Hara nodded. "I'll go along," he said.

When they entered Tanner's stateroom, everything appeared to be exactly as he had left it earlier, including Tanner's bloodied corpse on the bed. The captain stood for a moment looking down at the dead man, then pivoted to face O'Hara. He had lost his annoyance, and a grimly defeated look beclouded his features. "This is the first violent death on board the *Freebooty* since I assumed command three years ago," he said. "Coupled with the loss of the gold, it portends naught but disaster. The Pettibone brothers won't take kindly to such happenings, and mine is liable to be the first head on the block."

"We've not yet come into Stockton," O'Hara reminded him.

"You said it yourself, O'Hara—there are several hundred passengers and officers on board, and we have no idea which of them is guilty or of where to find the gold. A search of the steamer and all passengers before debarkation at Stockton would be impossible; some of these hotheaded miners and laborers we have on board would never stand still for it. We would have a riot on our hands."

"We've not yet come into Stockton," O'Hara repeated stolidly. "Now I'm thinking, Captain, that it would be wise if in the meanwhile you were to be confiding to no one the fact of Tanner's murder. Not even Mr. Woodman or Mr. Flucke."

"Well, I imagine you're right. The fewer people who are aware of it, the less chance there is of the news leaking out and alarming the passengers."

O'Hara said, "We've no need to be worrying about one of the stewards coming in with a passkey before we dock on the morrow, have we?"

"No. They come round to turn down the bedding and not again unless passengers request them to handle the luggage." The captain paused. "What do you intend to do next, O'Hara?"

"I've not yet decided," Fergus told him, which wasn't quite true.

"You'll keep me closely apprised, of course."

"Of course."

O'Hara left the packet master forward of the texas, walked aft along the larboard rail, reentered the texas from the opposite end, and used his borrowed set of master keys to lock the door to Number 14. All the while he pondered the captain's refusal to confide the nature of his after-supper activities. Was it because he, like Colfax, had arranged an assignation with one of the female passengers? That was possible; in addition to Miss Annabelle Thatch, O'Hara recalled from the list of texas passengers, there were two other women apparently traveling alone, both of whom bore the prefix of *Mrs.* Fifteen minutes or so, which was all the time the captain and Woodman had been apart, was little enough for proper trifling; still, a man of the captain's advanced years . . .

O'Hara passed by the doors of the two Mrs., and both showed lamplight from within. He debated the advisability of confronting each of them in turn, but without some evidence that the captain had indeed visited one of them, that would only be inviting adversity. And even though he could think of no other reason why the *Freebooty*'s master should be reluctant to explain his actions, the possibility could not be discounted that it was one of the couples or single male passengers in the other staterooms whom he had called on. Besides which, O'Hara had other, less nebulous matters to attend to.

Such as a thirst, he suddenly realized, that had grown prodigious and which was now demanding immediate attention.

⊱15⊰

The Saloon crowd had thinned considerably, although the room seemed no less noisy than it had on O'Hara's prior visits. Among those grouped at the buffet was the miner, who stood quaffing beer and eating fistfuls of salted nuts; the parrot was not perched on his shoulder, but Fergus spied it as he approached, crouched on the nearest table and glaring at a momentarily abandoned plug hat as though an old enemy were hiding inside.

O'Hara stood in next to the miner and ordered his customary pony of rye. Then, pretending sudden recognition, he said, "Well, you're the chap who was playing poker with Colfax earlier. Did you manage to turn the tables on him and win back some of your gold?"

The miner looked at him and made a grunting sound. He said, "Goddamned gamblers," reached for another handful of peanuts, lifted his mug and drained it and banged it down on the bar in what was evidently intended as a signal for a refill. In any case, one of the bartenders hurried up and took the mug away to the draught spigots.

Over on the table, the parrot jumped astraddle the hat. Clutching at opposite sides of the sweatband for balance, it wobbled there for a moment and then raised its tailfeathers. While it was doing that it seemed to become aware of being watched; it fixed its stare on O'Hara, and appeared to recognize him. "Night sign, men can too," it screeched nastily. "Son of a bitch." After which it lowered its tail, said "Ah" in a satisfied way, and hopped off the hat.

O'Hara said to the miner, "Impressive bird you have there."

"Goddamned nuisance, you mean," the miner said. "One of these days I'll wring its neck."

"It stays close to you, I've noticed."

"The hell it does. Stupid thing flies off all the time, looking for food or other birds to hump. Or just plain trouble. Got me into bad situations a time or two since I took it off a Chink at Angel's Camp. I ought to wring its Goddamned neck right now and be done with it."

"Horse dung," the parrot said.

"Cusses all the time, too," the miner said. He drank half of his fresh lager. "Be Goddamned if I know where the son of a bitch picked it up. Couldn't of been from the Chink."

"I saw it up in the texas a while ago," O'Hara said casually. "It was just flying out of a stateroom window, as a matter of fact—Mr. Tanner's stateroom."

Whatever reaction O'Hara had hoped this statement might elicit, it was not at all the one he got. The miner glowered not at him but at the parrot, and said, "Foraging again, I suppose. I catch you doing it one more time, I'll wring your Goddamn neck for certain."

Before either the parrot or O'Hara could say anything in response, an elegantly dressed silver-haired gentleman carrying a gold-knobbed cane came up to the table. The black plug hat apparently belonged to him; he reached out a hand and picked it up. The parrot glared up at him as the elegant gentleman said, "Well, what have we here? You're a handsome Polly, aren't you? Can you speak, Polly? What can you say?"

"In your hat, boss," the parrot said, "in your hat," and commenced to cackle insanely.

The elegant gentleman clamped the plug firmly on his head and walked away looking bewildered—which expression would probably not last much longer. The miner, meanwhile, slapped his knee as though the foregoing were an old joke (which perhaps it was), opened his mouth and threw back his head and allowed sounds of wild mirth to spill out.

Surprisingly, or possibly not so surprisingly, these sounds of wild mirth sounded just like the parrot's cackle.

O'Hara determined that there was no point in asking him further questions; it seemed obvious that the man was not guilty of anything other than playing with a short deck. He finished his rye in a swallow and left the pair of them cackling there together like scruffy witches on All Hallow's Eve.

He did not, however, leave the Saloon. He had noticed that while most of the gaming tables were either empty or occupied by several players, the one in the far corner was taken by only one man: John A. Colfax.

The gambler had a hand of solitaire spread out on the green felt in front of him, and his long-fingered hands skillfully maneuvered cards from pack to layout or to a separate, face-down pile. He was smiling faintly to himself, as if absorbed in some pleasant mental reflection. He did not look up until O'Hara had drawn out one of the facing chairs and seated himself, and his smile then changed shape and became less cordial than it had been at any of their previous meetings.

He said pointedly, "I don't wish to be rude, but I dislike sitting with someone at a card table unless there is a game in progress."

O'Hara chose to ignore that. He produced his pipe and began to fill it. "You're a good friend of Tanner's, are you not?" he asked in a mild way.

"Not particularly, no."

"It was my impression you were."

"Your impression is false. And why should you be interested in my relationship with Tanner?"

"It's my nature to be curious about a great many things."

"Poppycock."

"How did you happen to make Tanner's acquaintance?"

Colfax's hands stilled and his lips thinned; undisguised aggravation showed in his face. "Listen here, you've done nothing but ask questions of me each of the last three occasions we've met, and frankly I'm rather tired of it. What is it you're after, O'Hara?"

"Truth and honesty, same as most men."

"Well, I'll thank you to look for them elsewhere."

O'Hara smiled. "I could be taking that statement two ways, now couldn't I?"

Colfax slowly put down the pack of cards and said in a flat voice, "Good night, O'Hara."

Just as slowly, Fergus stood and thumbed a match into flame and began coaxing the pipe into a proper draw, all without taking his eyes off Colfax. The gambler met this scrutiny with a steady, inimical gaze of his own.

"Hello there, John, Mr. O'Hara," a cheerful voice said, and Horace T. Goatleg waddled up on O'Hara's left. He was balancing a small snack plate on which he had constructed an impressive architectural mound of cold cuts, relishes, three kinds of salad, several filberts and almonds, and an immense crowning fig. "Ah, these steamer repasts! The only item missing, it seems, is a barbecue of goat's leg." He rumbled in self-appreciation of his humor.

O'Hara and Colfax failed to smile or even glance in his direction; their eyes were still locked in visual combat. Goatleg's own smile weakened as he realized the tension, and he said, "Here, gentlemen, what's the trouble?" in a concerned tone.

"There's no trouble," Colfax said. "O'Hara was just leaving—weren't you, O'Hara?"

Deliberately, Fergus turned to the fat man. "You wouldn't happen to have seen Mr. Tanner since supper, would you?"

"Why, no, not a glimpse. Why?"

"I've been wanting a word with him," O'Hara said. "On a private matter. But he doesn't seem to be in his stateroom, and no one has seen him about."

Goatleg said, "Odd. Unless perhaps he retired early and is a sound sleeper. I am one myself, you know. One could pound on my door for ten minutes without rousing me from slumber."

"You're a close friend of the man, Mr. Goatleg?"

"Actually, no. We only met two weeks ago in San Francisco."

"Was that also when Colfax met Tanner?"

"Yes, but I—"

"And how long have you known Colfax?" O'Hara asked.

He had been calculating his questions to goad the gambler as much as to test and glean information from Goatleg, and Colfax had reached the limit of his endurance. He stood abruptly and put his right hand inside his coat; his cheeks were flushed with rage. "I've had all I can stand of you, O'Hara," he said. "Absolutely all."

"Calm yourself," Goatleg said. He looked perplexed and upset. "There's no need for harsh words, John—"

"There's need for more than that if he chooses to remain within my sight."

The fat man looked imploringly at O'Hara, who shrugged and said to Colfax, "I'll leave now—but I expect I'll be seeing you again before we dock at Stockton on the morrow."

"Not unless you care to court misadventure."

"As you like it," O'Hara said, and sauntered away at a leisurely pace. Inside, however, he was seething with repressed fury. His natural inclination had been to provoke the gambler further, in order to

see what he would do; but though his dislike of Colfax
had grown immeasurably, and he would have enjoyed
nothing more than to whittle on him with two good
Irish fists, O'Hara recognized the folly of that. Fisti-
cuffs at this juncture would serve no good purpose. As
well, Colfax doubtless carried a holdout weapon of
some kind inside his coat, as most gamblers were wont
to do, and thus there was the pointless danger of gun-
play. Time enough later to force the issue, should he
deem it profitable.

Out on deck again, O'Hara walked aft to the deserted deckhouse observation area. He stood at the
rail, in the shadows near the huge housing of the starboard paddlewheel, and reapplied flame to his pipe.
Beyond the near bank of the San Joaquin, a cluster of
farm buildings stood in the middle of the flat, moon-
drenched land, outlined against the starred sky and a
distant line of foothills; the impression was of a vivid
nocturnal painting, perfect in every detail. The chunking of the buckets lent a peacefully harmonious sound
to the night's serenity.

O'Hara immersed himself in thought. While ten
minutes passed and the cluster of farm buildings disappeared as the *Freebooty* traversed a bight in the
river, he reviewed everything he had seen and done
and heard in the past few hours. But none of it, by
damn, had produced a clue to the identity of the man
he sought, or to the whereabouts of the gold. . . .

Or had it?

Memory scraps, more than one, started to flicker
suddenly like guttering candles at the perimeter of his
mind—and then died before he could steady the
flames. A grim excitement touched him nonetheless;

there *were* clues, however insignificant or unrelated they might have seemed at the time, which he had noted and which had lodged in his subconscious. When he relighted those memory candles, at least part of the answer would be revealed, he was certain of—

Muffled sound behind him: bootsole sliding stealthily on the deck boarding.

Over the years O'Hara had developed an acute sensitivity to danger; he whirled about and dipped his body into a half-crouch, left hand fending in front of him and right hand sliding inside his coat for the Navy .36. He had a single, indistinct glimpse of a shadowy figure, heard a grunt of expelled breath and then a faint swishing sound that was by no means new to him.

The knife blade slashed downward at an angle, ripped through his upper right coat sleeve and stingingly into flesh. Slid free. The assailant's lunge pitched him into O'Hara, and both of them off-balance into the rail.

The thick wooden bar bit into the small of O'Hara's back, and because the attacker heaved free in that instant, it acted as a fulcrum. He felt his feet leave the deck and his body tilt into a horizontal position, teetering atop the rail. He flailed his arms and legs in a desperate effort to regain equilibrium and an upright stance, had a swift perception of the knife being raised again, realized there was only one way in which he could escape this second thrust, and jack-knifed backward over the rail just before the blade descended.

He had enough time to complete the midair somersault, and briefly to pray that there was no one and no obstruction directly beneath him on the main deck. Then his feet struck a flat, unyielding surface with bone-jarring impact, and pain erupted from soles to crotch, and a great ringing burst against his eardrums, and he felt himself sprawling, and—

Blank.

⊱16⊰

The first of O'Hara's senses to return was that of taste, and what he tasted in his mouth and throat was poteen.

He pried his eyes open, regained the sense of sight, and saw a ring of faces suspended above him, some of which belonged to members of the Mulrooney Guards and all of which were somewhat devilish in appearance, owing to the fact that they were bathed in the brassy light of at least two lanterns. The remainder of his senses returned simultaneously. Gone from his ears was the ringing, and he could hear well enough, but the sharp pain throughout his legs was still present, if a bit less severe; his right shoulder burned fiercely.

He was lying on the deck, he realized, and his head was propped up in a pair of strong hands. A familiar voice was saying, "It goes to show you, lads, what I've long stated for a fact: poteen's the only crature in the world that'll put you out and bring you to again, one as good as the other."

O'Hara blinked several times and moved his head slightly to focus on the face of Billy Culligan. The feisty little Mulrooney extended one of the earthenware jugs. "You'd best have another drap or two, O'Hara," he said. "It'll proper clear your brain."

The jug tilted against O'Hara's mouth.

Culligan said, "You come tumbling down direct at my feet and liked to startle the bejesus out of me." He bestowed a reproachful look on O'Hara. "You ought to have learned to hold your liquor a mite better—a healthy lad your age, and Irish besides."

The poteen had done its appointed task of properly clearing O'Hara's brain. He muttered a venomous oath and struggled into a sitting position, craning his neck for a look up at the deckhouse. There was, of course, no sign of the man who had attempted to kill him.

"God of Glory," one of the other Mulrooneys said, "will you look at the blood on the lad's arm. It's the blade of a knife done damage such as that, begob."

"A knife, is it?" Culligan said. "Was it that and not good drink that sent you over the rail, O'Hara?"

"Aye. Billy, did you see anyone peering down from up there after I came to a landing?"

"The glimpse of a man's face and shoulders, now that you ask of it; but he was gone in the flick of my eye. What happened up there? Were you set on by a bloody hooligan?"

O'Hara said that he had been, since it was the simplest explanation and one that required no elaboration.

"Would you be recognizing him again if you saw him?"

"It was too dark, and too quick in the happening."

"He didn't get your purse, did he?"

"No," O'Hara said. "Give me a hand up, lads."

When the men helped him to his feet, he found that he could stand unaided and with somewhat less pain than he had expected. He took a few experimental steps, hobbling like an old man with the gout; but this condition, he was sure, would only be temporary. He thanked the benevolence of St. Pat for having escaped the attack with no more than a gashed arm, and for not having broken a leg or even badly sprained one in the fall.

He inspected the knife wound. His coat sleeve and shirt sleeve beneath it had been rent from shoulder to elbow, but the cut itself was no more than the length of two fingers. It had bled considerably, though it seemed superficial enough; he still had full use of the limb. He removed his handkerchief and wrapped it around the wound, and one of the Mulrooneys stepped up with a second square of cloth to tie a makeshift bandage.

Culligan said, "You'd best have that cut washed and cleaned straightaway. Carbolic salve is what you'll be wanting to use, if your missus carries it."

"She does."

"You're able to navigate, now?"

"Aye."

"Well, you watch out for yourself," Culligan said. "And if you're in need of anything else, all you've to do is holler out the name Mulrooney."

O'Hara said he would, and limped around to the stairway and climbed slowly to the weather deck. It would not do to continue his investigation with his coat and shirt torn and bloody for all to see, which gave him no choice except to return to his and Hattie's stateroom immediately.

His legs were full of pricking needles by the time he entered the texas, and the edge of pain had begun to dull. He steeled himself for an encounter with Hattie, but to his relief he found the stateroom dark: she was evidently still in the Ladies' Cabin. He cleansed his arm, applied carbolic salve, wrapped it with gauze, changed into another of his suits and a clean shirt, hid the ruined garments under one of the bunkbeds, and left again—all within fifteen minutes. He was able to walk almost normally by then, with little pain.

Down to the Gentlemen's Saloon. Colfax and Goatleg were no longer at the gaming table and nowhere else in the room; O'Hara asked a random selection of waiters, bartenders and patrons if they could recall whether the gambler and the fat man had left together or separately, and when. None of them professed to be able to remember seeing Colfax and Goatleg at all.

Aft to the deckhouse observation area. Near the starboard rail he found his dropped pipe and tucked it away inside his pocket. There was nothing else in the vicinity which might point to the identity of his assailant. He paused for a moment, his back cautiously to the rail this time, and mentally reviewed the assault. The man, however, had been only a shadow, and he could not even recall the general size of him. He tried then to fetch up those memory scraps which had tantalized him just prior to the attack; but the brush with death had reburied them in his subconscious.

Up again to the weather deck, cursing under his breath, and back into the texas. He stopped in front of Number 8, which showed lampglow through the door louvers, and knocked sharply.

Goatleg's voice said, "Yes?"

"Fergus O'Hara, Mr. Goatleg."

Pause. "What is it you want at this late hour, sir?"

"Is Colfax there with you?"

"He is not."

"D'you know where he might be?"

"I do not."

The door opened and the fat man peered out. He wore an enormous striped nightshirt with a white linen napkin tucked into the collar; his upper lip was shiny with meat fat residue. Behind him O'Hara could see an empty plate and a coffee cup on the table, and that the stateroom was as empty of visitors named John A. Colfax as he had claimed.

O'Hara asked, "Did you and Colfax leave the Saloon immediately after my own departure?"

Goatleg frowned and looked considerably less jovial than at any time since O'Hara had met him. It seemed, Fergus thought without bother, that he was wearing out his welcome everywhere this night. "I left the Saloon shortly afterward, yes," the fat man said. "I came up here to eat my late meal."

"Colfax didn't leave with you?"

"No. See here, sir, Mr. Colfax told me of your constant questioning of him—and now you've come around with more of the same for me. What is the purpose of these Paul Pry activities?"

"I've a good one," O'Hara assured him blandly.

"Indeed? Well, I can't help wondering, sir, if you aren't something more—or less—than what you profess to be."

"Isn't everyone?" O'Hara said, and smiled—he felt more like grimacing, and perhaps howling, in frustration—and walked away before Goatleg could reply.

Forward, then, to the pilothouse. Bradley was at the wheel, kept company now by Titus Flucke; both men looked about nervously as O'Hara entered, relaxed again when they recognized him. The young pilot said, "You look fierce, Mr. O'Hara. Has something else happened?"

Fergus grunted. "What has become of Mr. Woodman?"

"He has gone to his quarters, I think. I'm feeling all right again, and he allowed me to take over the balance of my afterwatch."

"How long ago was it that he left you?"

"About forty-five minutes."

"And how long has Mr. Flucke been here?"

"Ten minutes or so," the purser said. He rubbed the Chinese-looking wart on his knobbly nose. "I wasn't able to sleep, and I thought a stroll and some conversation might help."

"So you were in your quarters an hour past?"

"I was."

"Have either of you seen the captain in that time?"

Bradley said, "He was here just after Mr. Woodman left."

"Did he tell you where he was about?"

"No, sir."

Out of the pilothouse and aft on the starboard. Woodman next, he thought—but he was fast realizing the futility of what he was doing. Seeking out his best suspects (if any, including Colfax, could be called that) and talking to them had not so far accomplished anything and was unlikely to; the guilty party, if indeed he spoke or had spoken to the guilty party, had only to tell him lies, and without some manner of evidence he had no way of discerning truth from falsehood.

If only he could remember and clarify one of those tantalizing clues. . . .

He reached the aft stairway, started past it, and then stopped. Below, the captain was just heading up from the deckhouse with a small bundle clutched beneath the fold of his coat, as though for purposes of concealment. He was looking back over his shoulder at the moment, and his overall manner was rather furtive.

O'Hara stepped back just as the captain began to swing his gaze up the staircase, and moved quickly into the deep shadows alongside the gallows A-frame of the walking-beam. Perhaps the captain was only on his way to his quarters, or back to the pilothouse; but perhaps, too, he was bound elsewhere, such as to the texas stateroom he had visited carrying another small bundle after supper.

When he reached the weather deck the captain paused to glance in both directions, then came farther aft and around the corner of the texas without seeing O'Hara. He entered the tunnel. The moment he was out of sight, O'Hara hastened over to the outer texas wall, put his back to it and eased his head out to look down the length of the corridor. The *Freebooty*'s master had slowed to a near standstill at the center of the tunnel, and now he took something from his pocket—a key?—and went diagonally to the door of one of the starboard staterooms. Number 11, O'Hara judged, which the texas passenger list said was unoccupied this trip.

The captain glanced to forward, and O'Hara immediately pulled his head out of the entranceway. He counted to five, after which he chanced another look. The packet master was now facing the stateroom door, working at the latch with the key. An instant later the door opened and he vanished inside.

O'Hara rubbed his hands together in an anticipatory way, put the right one inside his coat and onto the butt of his Navy .36, and walked rapidly but silently down the tunnel to Number 11. Lamplight showed behind the closed door. He put his ear against the louvered panel: he could hear voices within, at least two of them, but the conversation was being conducted in soft tones, and he was unable to distinguish more than an occasional word.

Overt action, he decided, was called for at this stage. Carefully he depressed the latch handle until he heard a click, which told him the captain had not relocked the bolt from within, and then he drew the Navy revolver and shoved against the door and stepped inside the cabin.

The two occupants froze, staring at him. The captain stood with one hip resting against the table; the second man, a scrawny, wizened individual, lay propped up on one of the bunkbeds—and he looked as though he had been kicked and trod upon by several teams of horses. Both eyes were blackened and his face and bare chest were covered with a variety of bruises, abrasions and contusions which ran the color spectrum from a hideous lemon-brown to an interesting bluish mauve. His expression was difficult to fathom for all of this, but O'Hara thought it contained a combination of surprise, fear and resignation.

The captain's own surprise modulated into anger.

"Damn you, O'Hara, what are you doing here! I told you my visit to the texas after supper could have no bearing on other events!"

Fergus closed the door and leaned back against it. Since neither of the other two seemed inclined toward violence (the scrawny individual did not even look capable of it at the moment), he held the gun loosely pointed at the floor; that gave him a relaxed, even careless pose—deliberately. He said, "So you did, Captain. But I've come for proof of it."

The scrawny individual asked, "Uh—who are you?" without opening his mouth more than a quarter inch, possibly because he was not able to open his mouth more than a quarter inch.

"Fergus O'Hara. The captain hasn't told you of what has been happening tonight?"

"I . . . I haven't seen him since he brought me supper."

"Supper?" O'Hara looked with some disappointment at the two plates, utensils, and coffee cup—and remains of food—on a folded white linen cloth on the table. "Bundled nicely in that tablecloth, no doubt."

The captain took a step toward him. Fergus motioned with the Navy .36, and the captain halted. O'Hara said, "Now why would you be smuggling supper to this gentleman? Why couldn't the steward be bringing it?" He tugged meditatively at his beard with his left hand. "Well, no doubt because he has no business being in a stateroom listed as unoccupied. Or on the *Freebooty* at all."

The captain's cheeks suffused with color; he said nothing.

O'Hara said, "And why would you be a party to such as that, Captain? Because he's a felon, perhaps, and you're helping him to flee from the authorities—?"

"No! He is *not* a felon."

"What is he, then?"

"A prospector—and my brother, Aaron."

O'Hara raised an eyebrow.

"Oh, all right," the captain said, "there's no point in trying to keep anything from you—I can see that now. But I'll demand your promise first not to repeat a word of what I tell you if you're satisfied it has nothing to do with the theft of the gold. What I've done is unethical, if understandable in the circumstances, and would doubtless cost me my position if the Pettibone brothers were to catch wind of it. Not that I'm sanguine about keeping my position anyway, after all that has happened tonight." He said the last dejectedly.

O'Hara said, "My only interest is what has happened tonight."

"Very well." The captain glanced at his brother, who was looking bewildered as well as frightened (but no longer resigned). "O'Hara is a detective, Aaron. We've had a shipment of gold stolen tonight from the safe in the pilothouse. I'll explain about that later."

When Aaron nodded nervously, the captain said to Fergus, "Well, you're right, of course, that Aaron has no business being in this stateroom; he did not even pay deck steerage. As a matter of fact, I had him taken on board in my private trunk. He was in no condition to walk, and besides that, both he and I wanted to make certain no one knew he had left San Francisco."

— 161 —

"Why not?"

"Certain individuals are after him."

"What individuals?"

"A Miss Lucinda Brighthaven and two of her relatives. She has it in her head that Aaron has hoarded a fortune in dust from a mine he worked a year ago in the Mother Lode. Near Koontzville."

"She tried to get me to marry her at first," Aaron said, "but I'm not the marrying kind; never have been, never will be. Then she started threatening me, and I figured it was time to leave Koontzville. Mine was about worked out anyway. So I came to San Francisco, figured I'd stay a spell and visit with Leland here before moving on. Only Lucinda followed me and brought those two relatives of hers with her."

"And they beat you," O'Hara said.

"No," Aaron said, "they only held me. Lucinda did all this herself. Damned strong woman, and mean as a whisky fart in Sunday church."

"Did you notify the police?"

"I did," Aaron said. "Didn't do me any good. Lucinda and her relatives claimed I attacked 'em first and they was only protecting their own selves. I couldn't prove no different. She had the relatives watching me every minute after that, and as broken up as I am I couldn't get away from 'em for long on my own; so I asked Leland to help me before they came after me again, which is just what they would of done first chance they had."

O'Hara said, "Bah."

Aaron blinked. The captain said angrily, "I suppose you don't believe Aaron's story. Damn it, man, it's the truth!"

"That's the bloody trouble," O'Hara said. He went over to where the bundle the captain had been carrying tonight lay unopened on the other bunkbed. He loosened it and spread the cloth: more potables from the riverboat's galley, undoubtedly intended to be breakfast fare, since the captain would be too busy in the morning to attend to food-smuggling chores.

O'Hara grimaced and put the revolver away. He opened the wardrobe and looked inside, but it was only a gesture; and of course the wardrobe was empty.

"Well?" the captain said.

"I've not even been inside this stateroom tonight. I don't know you've a brother named Aaron, and I've never in my life heard of a Miss Lucinda Bright-haven—although she sounds suspiciously like a madam I once knew casually in Saint Louis."

The captain looked relieved. Aaron looked relieved.

O'Hara looked disgusted. "Bah," he said again, and opened the door and resisted the urge to slam it shut behind him as he stalked out.

-17-

Hattie said, "You may as well admit it, Fergus: you've no more idea now than at the beginning who murdered Mr. Stuart and Mr. Tanner and stole the consignment of gold—and no way left to find out."

"I'll admit nothing of the kind," O'Hara said. "Hattie, I tell you I've seen and heard enough throughout this business to *know* who it is I'm after, and perhaps even where the gold is to be found this very minute. If only I could be fetching up a single one of those clues, and examining it, the others will fall directly into place. I'm certain of it."

"Mightn't these 'clues' be little more than wishful thinking?" she asked mildly.

"They might not, confound it. Blast this detecting business! If Allan Pinkerton were here at this moment—"

"—you would ask his advice and guidance."

"Bah."

"Of course, you could always retire from the profession."

"Bah," O'Hara said again, and picked up his

banjo and began strumming random chords from "Kathleen Mavourneen."

It was now well past 2:00 A.M.,and they were in their stateroom—O'Hara fully dressed and seated on his bunkbed, Hattie in her nightgown and in her bed. She had been waiting for him when he returned a few minutes earlier, and she had not learned anything further of relevance from Mrs. Yount or anyone else in the Ladies' Cabin. She had noticed immediately that he was wearing different clothing, but she had not found the bloody coat and shirt under his bunk; so he had fabricated a tale of a drunken passenger spilling beer over him in the Saloon ("Beer again," she had said wearily), and he had silently vowed to sleep with his shirt on tonight and inform her of the knife wound tomorrow or possibly next week.

He had confided everything else, however, including the sagas of Miss Annabelle Thatch and of the captain and his brother Aaron. And her general reaction of a moment ago was understandable, if not in the least heartening. He *didn't* appear to have anywhere else to go, any way to determine the truth; he had run out of questions to ask, and he had nothing tangible with which to separate truth from prevarication. (As a further example of this, he had knocked on Woodman's door after leaving Number 11, and the chief pilot had refused him admittance—had in fact used rather abusive language in telling O'Hara to remove himself and not to interrupt his, Woodman's, sleep again unless he had found the gold or the man who had stolen it. Which man may have been Woodman himself, but O'Hara hadn't said so; he had been so frustrated that he had only walked away.)

The ironic fact, of course, was that those elusive clues *were* genuine and *would* tell him exactly where to go and what to do in order to find his man and the gold. They would answer everything. And he could not grasp hold of a single one. Not one!

Hattie put out the lamp, and because she had had her say and knew enough now to leave him alone—and because she had the uncanny ability to sleep at any time and anywhere, such as in the middle of an Indian massacre—she promptly went to sleep.

Not one.

O'Hara stopped playing the banjo when the tips of his fingers became sore. Then he just sat there in the dark, brooding and listening for surreptitious sounds from outside the door or window in the perverse hope that his man intended to make yet another attempt on his life. But there were no sounds and no attempt, and the Navy .36 remained under the blanket at his side.

Not one.

The cabin began to lighten and the steamer to stir with new activity: dawn.

And not one, not one, not one . . . .

⊷18⊷

When the *Freebooty* came out of the last of the
snakelike bends in the river and started down the last
long reach to Stockton, Hattie and O'Hara were sitting
at one of the tables near the starboard deckhouse rail,
opposite the entrance to the Social Hall. It was just
past seven-thirty—a spring-crisp, cloudless St.
Patrick's Day morning—and the steamer would dock
in another thirty minutes.

O'Hara was in a foul humor: three-quarters angry
frustration and one-quarter lack of sleep. He had left
the stateroom at six o'clock and had gone up to the
pilothouse and found the captain, Woodman, and
Bradley drinking coffee thickened with molasses.
Their humors had not been much better than his, and
there had been little conversation; O'Hara, in fact, had
divined that as a result of his failure to perform as
advertised, coupled with his less than ingratiating investigative techniques, he had fallen into general
disfavor—which fact decided him to stay on for two
cups of coffee instead of one. He saw no reason why
they should be allowed to suffer in any way less than
he.

Then he had prowled the decks for a time, without incident and without encountering such of his suspects as Colfax or Goatleg or the miner, and finally returned to the stateroom. Hattie had been up and dressed by then, and had attempted and failed to lighten his mood with sprightly comments. When she broached the subject of breakfast, he had told her growlingly that he had no damned appetite—a gauge of the depth of his depression, since he seldom spoke to her in any but the gentlest of tones.

Now he sat puffing on his briar and scowling at the passengers who walked or were seated nearby. Across from him Hattie was absorbed in *Elsie Venner,* which irrationally upset him further because he felt she ought, for the sake of wifely sympathy, to be as despondent as he was. Even the fact that this was St. Pat's Day failed in the slightest to cheer him; he was beginning to wonder if perhaps Pat had decided to punish past transgressions (of which there were several, he had to admit) by ignoring his present predicament.

From overhead, suddenly, there was a squawking sound, and the parrot swooped down in a gaudy swirl of red, green, yellow and blue, and came to a fluttering perch on the rail. It stared down at the slow-moving river frothed by the huge churning sidewheel, and apparently was not impressed by what it saw. It hopped about to look round the deck, spied O'Hara, made a cackling noise, and flew over to land on the back of an empty chair at their table.

"Take no chances," the bird said. "Men can too."

O'Hara was in no frame of mind for avian nonsense. He gave it a basilisk stare twice as evil as its own, and the parrot shuddered—or at least shook its feathers in the appearance of a shudder—and promptly tucked its head under its wing.

Hattie had lowered her book and was frowning thoughtfully. "What was that the bird said?"

O'Hara grunted.

The parrot, however, took its head out from under its wing and obligingly said, "Men can too. Night sign. Bollocks on a bull."

"Fergus," Hattie said, "didn't I hear the unlewd of those phrases last night while both you and it were in Tanner's stateroom?"

"I expect you did. What does it matter?"

"Well, judging from the balance of its vocabulary, no doubt learned from the miner and others like him, don't phrases such as 'night sign' and 'men can too' strike you as a bit odd?"

O'Hara said, "Not especially," but no sooner were the words past his lips that he realized what Hattie was getting at. He sat up straighter in his chair. "You're thinking the bird might be repeating phrases overheard in that stateroom—phrases perhaps spoken by the murderer."

"It's possible, isn't it?"

"Aye. Aye, it is." He stared at the parrot, much less malevolently now. "Night sign," he said. "Men can too. Take no chances. Night sign."

"Goddamn," the parrot said. It muttered something in Chinese and flew off the chair and disappeared above: another reluctant questionee.

O'Hara echoed the second half of the bird's last comment in English, though not aloud. He stood abruptly. He could feel his mind turning, his thoughts shifting as though searching for a proper order in which to settle. Muted excitement replaced some of the moody dejection. The answer *wanted* to take shape now—not just one of the clues, but all of them together to form a complete pattern. . . .

He paced away from the table without realizing what he was doing or where he was going, trance-like—and shortly ran into someone. He said "Uff," and the someone said dryly, "Well, it's Mr. O'Hara again," and he blinked and saw that it was the bushy-haired newspaperman.

"A fine morning," the reporter said conversationally. His eyes were red-veined and he looked altogether as hungover as he had yesterday. This did not seem to have had any effect on his cheerful disposition, however.

O'Hara made another of his grunting sounds and detoured around him to the rail. The newspaperman either did not know or did not care that he had been rather rudely dismissed; he joined O'Hara, leaning companionably on the rail.

"I should have kept my own counsel last night," he said, "and not had anything more to drink. Unfortunately, I have a fondness for the social drink—one of my sadder vices. But then, a man may have no bad habits and have worse."

O'Hara grunted again.

The reporter looked out at the broad, yellowish land of the San Joaquin Valley, beyond the cottonwood-lined bank; then he lowered his gaze to the river. "Clear as a mirror, isn't it?" he said. "It reminds me of the Mississippi when I was a boy, and of how we would swim bare on mornings such as this. Even the strapping we would sometimes get for doing it seemed worthwhile."

O'Hara, who had turned and been even more rudely prepared to walk away, pivoted back and jerked into a rigid posture, as though someone had caught hold of his coat collar. He stood that way for several seconds, oblivious to the startled look of the newspaperman. At length he said explosively, "By damn! By damn, now!"

"What is it, O'Hara?"

Fergus's eyes, bright and glittering now, shifted to the bushy-haired man, and he clapped him exuberantly on the shoulder. "Lad, it may yet be a fine morning after all. It may yet be, indeed."

He spun away before the newspaperman could respond. Hattie was standing at the table, frowning over at him; he made a staying gesture in passing and hurried down to the aft stairway. The zeal pulsing in him now had obliterated all of his foul humor, for he had the answer at last—all of it, all the clues having sprung vividly into his mind, as though chain-linked together, to create the solution to the mystery. What had been required was a key, and after Hattie's perceptive comments on the parrot had oiled the latch of his memory, the reporter's nostalgic remarks had at last unlocked it. Not a moment too soon, either, he thought. Aye, not a moment too soon. . . .

On the weather deck, he moved aft of the texas and stopped directly before the gallows frame of the walking-beam. There was no one else in the immediate vicinity. O'Hara stepped up as close to the frame as he was able and put his head and both arms carefully inside the vent opening, avoiding the machinery of the massive piston. Heat and the heavy odor of cylinder oil assailed him; the throb of the piston was very loud.

He felt along the interior walls of the frame, his fingertips encountering a greasy buildup of oil and dust. After a moment, high on the left side, they also encountered a fairly large metal hook which had been screwed into the wood. There was nothing suspended from the hook at present, but O'Hara knew that there had been during most of the night.

The gold, of course.

And he was fairly certain where it could now be found.

When he withdrew his head and arms from the vent opening, there was grease on his hands and on his coat and shirt sleeves, and he was sweating from the heat. He used his handkerchief, and then hastened across to the rear of the texas and paused in front of the cabin he wanted. The man who occupied these quarters was likely to be elsewhere at the moment, but it was a situation that called for complete caution. O'Hara put his right hand inside his coat and took hold of the revolver; with his left he rapped softly on the panel.

There was no response.

He knocked again, waited, concluded the cabin was indeed empty, and removed from his coat the set of master keys which he had not gotten around to returning to the purser's office. Just as he had done last night, at these same quarters, he slipped quickly inside and shut the door behind him.

He looked around briefly and settled on the wardrobe as the most likely of locations. Inside, in addition to the few articles of clothing he had previously sifted through, were two items of considerable import: a wide leather belt ornamented with bronze war-issue coins, and an Indian-beaded poke that contained a bill-fold which in turn contained papers and documents belonging to Charles Tanner. These papers and documents fitted the last piece of the puzzle together for O'Hara.

He tucked the poke into his coat pocket, then began to search the remainder of the cabin. It took him exactly three minutes to find the greasy calfskin grip hidden beneath the single bunkbed and behind a large open-topped wooden tool carrier. He drew the bag out, worked at the locked catch with one of the blades of his penknife, and got it open.

The gold was there, in two-score small pouches.

O'Hara looked at the sacks for several seconds, smiling. But then he found himself thinking of the captain, and of the bank in Stockton which urgently awaited the consignment. He sobered, shaking himself mentally; this was neither the time nor the place for rumination, and there was still much to be done. He refastened the grip, hefted it, and started to rise.

And the cabin door burst open and the man whose quarters these were, the man who had murdered Thomas Stuart and Charles Tanner and who had stolen the gold, stood framed in the entranceway. The junior pilot, Bradley.

⊷19⊶

Bradley was trembling, his face taut with fear and rage, his left hand knotted into a fist and his right clenched around the buckhorn grip of a Bowie knife. "So you found out, did you?" he said. "You damned Pinkerton meddler!"

And he launched himself across the cabin.

O'Hara had had the calfskin grip in his right hand and had started to transfer it to his left, but he had no time to draw his revolver, or even to set himself properly against the rush. All he could do was to sidestep the slashing knife and thrust the grip out in front of him in the manner of a shield. Bradley veered in the same direction without checking momentum. The knife sliced air, but his shoulder struck the grip and drove it back into O'Hara's chest. Both men then hit the larboard bulkhead with sufficient force to dislodge a small, faded oil painting.

O'Hara went to his knees, releasing the grip, and then skittered away as Bradley raked wildly with the knife. He fetched himself onto his feet, staggering against the center table, using it for leverage. When he regained his balance, Bradley was standing too, with the Bowie extended out from his body, palm turned upward. The curved "gullet tickler" at the end of the blade gleamed wickedly.

They stood motionless, facing each other across a distance of six feet. O'Hara had already discarded the idea of making a further effort to draw the Navy, for if he did, Bradley would strike immediately—and a knife blade was far swifter, far deadlier than a handgun in these circumstances, even if he could manage to free the revolver.

With forced calm he said, "The game's up, lad; you should be knowing that now. You'll make matters easier for yourself by dropping that knife and surrendering."

"I'll drop it inside *you,*" Bradley said shrilly. "Just as I would have done last night if you weren't such a damned lucky Irishman. I'll not hang for murder."

There was nothing to be gained, then, O'Hara thought, by further attempts at reason; Bradley was too frightened and too desperate. He watched the young pilot ease forward, moving the Bowie in slow concentric circles across his body. Frightened and desperate, aye—but not so much so that he had lost his cunning altogether. After that first wild attack he seemed to have realized that he was facing no ordinary foe, and that understanding made him all the more dangerous and difficult to disarm.

O'Hara did not look at Bradley's face as he advanced; you could not defend yourself against such as a Bowie knife by watching anything but that weapon, as he had learned well enough in the Irish Channel in his youth. Inside him, black fury raged for the indignities Bradley had suffered on him these past two days, and was suffering on him at this moment. He stood his ground, forcing his muscles to remain untensed but giving the outward impression of paralysis. The younger man's fingers were loose around the knife handle, and O'Hara stared at them, waiting, because when Bradley essayed his thrust, the fingers would tighten in reflex a fraction of a second early.

The sound of their breathing was harsh and unnaturally sibilant in the confines of the cabin, and sweat flowed thickly under O'Hara's arms and along his sides. He could feel the beginnings of a tic below his left eye, but he dared not blink. Just that much time might give Bradley all the advantage he would need—

The fingers tightened; the young pilot made a low sound in his throat and lunged upward with the knife.

O'Hara twisted to one side, drawing in his not insubstantial stomach and arching his back so that his body formed a rough letter C. The underhand slash cut through the material of his frock coat, and the Bowie hung up there. He caught Bradley's wrist in his left hand and the elbow in his right and brought his knee up and the youth's arm down in the same motion. There was a thin cracking sound, and Bradley cried out in pain; the knife slid free of O'Hara's coat, fell clattering to the floor. O'Hara kicked it across the cabin.

But there was still fight left in the junior pilot, an even greater desperation now that his right arm had been disabled. His booted foot struck O'Hara's shin, eliciting a bellow of pain and a half-strangled Anglo-Saxonism, and then he pitched himself head down into O'Hara and they reeled drunkenly together, Fergus struggling to disengage himself long enough to deliver a culminating blow.

Then his calves hit the edge of the bunk, and he spilled backward across it and banged his head solidly on the rounded projection of wood which served as a headboard.

Black streaks blurred his vision. Bradley was sprawled across him, whimpering, swinging frenziedly with his good arm. The forearm O'Hara put up only partially succeeded in warding off the blows, and one finally connected with his bearded jaw. The black streaks fused into a shimmering ebony wall.

He was still conscious, but he seemed to have momentarily lost all power of movement. The flailing weight that was Bradley lifted from him. There were scuffling sounds. The knife, O'Hara thought—but Bradley either couldn't locate the weapon or had decided in his panic that he would not be able to handle O'Hara using his left hand only. There was the sharp running slap of his boots receding across the cabin and on the deck outside.

O'Hara's jaw and the back of his head began a simultaneous and painful throbbing, and mobility returned seconds later. Shaking his head to clear his vision, he swung off the bunk, stumbling as pain flamed in the shin Bradley had kicked, and let loose with a many-jointed oath which even his grandfather, who had always sworn he could out-cuss the devil himself, would have been proud to call his own. When he could see again, he realized that Bradley had caught up the calfskin grip and taken it with him. Then he hobbled to the door and turned to larboard out of it, the way the running steps had gone.

Bradley, hampered by the weight and bulk of the grip, his right arm flopping uselessly at his side, was at the bottom of the aft stairway when O'Hara reached the top. He glanced upward, saw the unexpected proximity of pursuit, and began to run feverishly toward the nearby main-deck staircase. He banged into passengers, scattering them; whirled a fat woman around like a ballerina executing a pirouette, and sent the reticule she had been carrying sailing gracefully over the rail and into the river below.

Men commenced calling in angry voices and milling about as O'Hara came tumbling down the stairs to the deckhouse. At the top of the main-deck staircase a burly individual in denim stepped suddenly in front of Bradley, who did not see him until it was too late for him to do anything except crash into the other man. Both toppled sprawling to the deck.

O'Hara would have caught Bradley then had it not been for the intervention of the thin, horse-faced woman in crinoline and lace (she ought to have been in a harness and blinders, O'Hara might have thought had he had time for such reflections). She came hurrying around the corner from the observation area aft of the Ladies' Cabin, doubtless to see what all the commotion was about, and O'Hara charged into her in much the same way Bradley had charged into the burly man. They also went down asprawl, and the horse-faced woman made a sound that was an odd combination of a screech and a neigh, and her skirts and petticoats billowed high around her waist—and O'Hara, through no fault of his own, ended up with his head trapped in the vicinity of her upper thighs as the crinoline and lace settled again.

The horse-faced woman screech-neighed as though she had been mortally wounded—perhaps in a way she had been—and kneed O'Hara in the nose. Then she flailed at him with hard little fists. It so happened that his struggles worked in direct opposition to hers, again through no fault of his own, which meant that it took him longer to get his head out from under her skirts and his body away from her knees and fists than it should have.

He sat up shaking his head, and she sat up screeching and neighing, and a horse-faced man of approximately the same age and size as the woman said in a morally outraged, if timed, nicker, "Here, what do you think you're *doing!* That happens to be my wife, sir!"

"No question of that," O'Hara said under his breath, and heaved himself to his feet. "And you're welcome to her, sir."

"Shoot him, Wyatt!" the woman screeched. "He's a fiend; he's a spawn of the devil!"

Wyatt took a closer look at O'Hara and said, "Uh."

O'Hara was looking over at the main-deck staircase. Bradley had gotten up, he saw, and the burly man hadn't; Bradley, in fact, was just starting down the stairs.

"He touched my body!" the woman neighed. "Kill him, Wyatt! Beat him down with your fists! Wyatt? Wyatt, you coward, come back here—!"

O'Hara limped to the staircase, one hand pressed against his nose where the horse-faced woman had kneed him. He got there just in time to see Bradley bowl over two startled Chinese below as though they were bundles of sticks. When he himself descended, Bradley was racing toward the taffrail and looking back over his shoulder as he did so. O'Hara thought: The damned fool is about to jump into the river! And when he does, the weight of the gold will take the bag straightway to the bottom, and him with it—

All at once he became aware that there were not very many passengers currently inhabiting the aft section of the main deck, when there should have been a veritable mass of them. Some of those who were present had heard the commotion on the upper deck and been drawn to the staircase; the rest were split into two groups, one lining the larboard rail and the other lining the starboard, and their attention was held by a different spectacle. Some of these were murmuring excitedly; others looked amused; and still others appeared mildly apprehensive. The center section of the deck directly opposite the taffrail was completely cleared.

The reason was suddenly and abundantly obvious to O'Hara. A small, rusted, and very old half-pounder had been set up on wooden chocks at the taffrail, aimed downriver like an impolitely pointing finger.

Beside the cannon was a keg of black powder and a charred-looking ramrod.

And surrounding the cannon were the Mulrooney Guards, one of whom held a firebrand poised above the fuse vent and all of whom were now loudly singing "The Wearing of the Green."

O'Hara knew in that moment what it was the Mulrooney Guards had had secreted inside their wooden crate, and why they had been so anxious to get it aboard quickly and without having the contents examined; and he knew the meaning of Billy Culligan's remark about planning to "start off St. Pat's Day with a mighty salute." He stopped running and opened his mouth to shout at Bradley, who was still fleeing and still looking back over his shoulder, and at the Mulrooney Guard with the firebrand. He could not recall afterward if he actually *did* shout or not; if so, it was something akin to tossing a burning match into a bonfire.

The Mulrooney cannoneer touched off the fuse. The other Mulrooney Guards scattered, still singing. The watching passengers huddled farther back, some averting their eyes. Bradley kept on running toward the taffrail.

And the cannon, as well as the keg of black powder, promptly and deafeningly blew up.

ᐻ20ᐸ

The *Freebooty* lurched and rolled with the sudden
concussion, and a great sweeping cloud of sulfurous
black smoke enveloped the riverboat. O'Hara caught
hold of one of the uprights in the starboard rail and
clung to it, coughing and choking. They used too much
powder and not enough bracing, he thought. Then
he thought: Now I hope Hattie had the good sense
to stay where she was on the deckhouse.

The steamer was in a state of bedlam: everyone
on each of the three decks screaming or shouting.
Some of the passengers thought a boiler had exploded
—a common enough steamboat hazard—and it was
a while before they stopped believing their lives
were in danger from a second explosion. When the
smoke finally began to dissipate, O'Hara looked in the
direction of the center taffrail and discovered that
most of it, like the cannon, was missing. The deck in
that area was blackened and scarred, some of the
boarding torn into splinters.

But there did not seem to have been any casual-
ties. A few people had received minor injuries, most of

those being Mulrooney Guards, and several were speckled with black soot; none of the passengers, however, had fallen overboard, and none had been seriously scorched by the exploding powder. Even Bradley had miraculously managed to survive the concussion, despite his proximity to the cannon when it and the powder keg had gone up. He was moaning feebly and moving his arms and legs, looking like a bedraggled chimney sweep, when O'Hara got to him.

The grip containing the gold had faired somewhat better. Bradley had been shielding it with his body at the moment of the blast, and while it was torn open and the leather pouches scattered about, most of the sacks were intact. One or two had split open, and particles of the gold dust glittered in the sooty air. The preponderance of passengers were too concerned with their own welfare to notice; those who did stared disbelievingly but kept their distance, because no sooner had O'Hara reached Bradley and the gold than the captain and half a dozen of the deck crew arrived.

"Bradley?" the captain said. "My God, *Bradley's* the one who stole the gold?"

"Aye, he's the one."

"Woodman will have apoplexy when he learns of it. Pilots are above reproach, in his estimation." The captain seemed dazed and therefore inclined to ramble a bit; he appeared enormously relieved that the dust had been recovered, and at the same time chagrined over the identity of the thief and what had happened to the aft, main deck section of his palatial steamer. He blinked at O'Hara. "That commotion just before the explosion, the report of one man chasing another—that was you after Bradley,

O'Hara? You had somehow discovered he was the thief?''

O'Hara said it was, and that he had, and explained briefly what had transpired in Bradley's quarters. He noticed as he spoke that several of the passengers from the upper decks had come down and were staring at Bradley and the gold, murmuring among themselves. Included in this group were Hattie—who appeared to have weathered the explosion without damage, and who looked a little bewildered—and the newspaperman, Goatleg, Colfax, the miner, and on the miner's shoulder, the parrot.

The captain had enough presence of mind to order the deckhands to attend to Bradley and to gather up the pouches of dust. Then O'Hara drew him to one side. Speaking softly, he said, ''Bradley is also the skalpeen who murdered Charles Tanner last night, and did in a man by the name of Thomas Stuart in San Francisco two nights ago. Stuart, you see, was an employee of the California Merchants Bank, and I expect in league with Bradley.''

The captain grappled with this for a moment and then nodded. ''So that is how he knew of the gold shipment.''

''It is. But, you understand, Bradley and Stuart weren't the only two conjoined in the plot.''

''You mean there's a *gang* of thieves involved?''

''You might say that. But I'm thinking of one other man specifically.''

''What man?''

O'Hara turned, surveyed the crowd for a few seconds, then moved toward the larboard rail. He stopped finally and tapped a bulging vest with his forefinger, not lightly.

"This man," he said. "Horace T. Goatleg."

Goatleg, who had been well out of earshot of their conversation, looked at him in a warily puzzled way. The captain's expression was still one of astonishment as he came up. The other passengers, sensing that some further drama was about to take place, parted away from the three men; they grew silent, watching expectantly.

"Just what did you mean by 'this man,' sir?" Goatleg said.

O'Hara said flatly, "That you're the one behind the theft of that gold yonder, and behind a pair of murders as well."

The passengers made a collective gasping sound and moved farther back. Goatleg stared at O'Hara and then opened his mouth and allowed the familiar rumbling sound to issue forth; the laughter, however, did not touch his narrowed eyes. "You must be daft, O'Hara," he said. "I know nothing about that gold, and certainly nothing about any murders."

"I've been acquainted with Mr. Goatleg for more than a year," the captain said. "Why, he's a respectable citizen and a gentleman."

"I might have thought so myself until recently."

"But why would *he* stoop to gold thievery? He possesses considerable wealth—"

"Does he, now? Well, you can't be saying the same for the Confederate States at this point in the war, can you?"

"The Confederate States?"

"Goatleg is not only a blackguard and a murderer but a member—and a high-ranking one, I'll warrant—of the Knights of the Golden Circle."

The passengers began murmuring again, and there

was an ominous stirring among the sooty members of the Mulrooney Guards. Goatleg attempted to adopt a posture of righteous indignation; his eyes, however, were like bits of gray stone imbedded in frost.

He said, "You definitely are a lunatic, sir. Only a madman could conceive of such preposterous nonsense."

The captain's gaze swiveled between the two men. "Are you absolutely certain of these allegations, O'Hara?"

"I am. And I've proof to be backing 'em up."

"Faugh!" Goatleg said. "What proof?"

"The gambler, Colfax, to begin with."

"Colfax? An acquaintance, nothing more."

"Except a fellow Knight of the Golden Circle."

Colfax, standing a few paces on Goatleg's right, was startled; he recovered enough to say "That's a lie," but the words lacked the conviction of truth.

"There are documents which verify it," O'Hara lied. "And I expect you knew of the plot to steal the gold, if not of the murders as well. You can be hanged the same as Goatleg."

The gambler, all at once and to O'Hara's satisfaction, lost his suavity and self-possession. He looked around nervously as people began drawing away from him; sweat popped out on his brow. "I . . . I've had nothing to do with murder," he said.

"None of us have had anything to do with murder," Goatleg said. "O'Hara has offered *no* proof of any wrongdoing on my part or on yours. None whatsoever."

"There's Charles Tanner for that."

Goatleg's eyes became as narrow as gunslits.

Colfax said, "What does Tanner have to do with it?"

"Everything—as a United States Revenue agent."

"What's that?" the captain said. "Good God—"

Goatleg said, "If that is true, it comes as a surprise."

"Aye, I expect it did—last night."

"I learned of it then—is that your contention?"

"It is."

"And killed him for that reason, I suppose?"

O'Hara smiled coldly. "Killed him, did you say? Well now, that's an interesting comment, considering that only the captain and myself knew that Tanner was killed last night. How did you know it yourself, Goatleg, if you didn't have a hand in the deed?"

There was a frozen moment: heavy, tense. Then the fat man, realizing he had entrapped himself, reacted with such swiftness that O'Hara was caught flatfooted. His hand flashed inside his frock coat and flashed out again with a double-barreled Remington derringer; he backed away against the rail, holding the weapon pointed at O'Hara's midsection. One of the women passengers screamed softly. Hattie's voice said "Fergus!" and the captain said "Damn!" and there was a backward crush of bodies. Only O'Hara, the captain, Colfax, and Goatleg—and the contingent of Mulrooney Guards—stood motionless.

"You're a fool if you think that little holdout gun will buy your freedom," O'Hara said. "You've only two bullets in it, and once you use 'em, you'll be trampled."

"If I'm forced to use them, you may be sure it will

be on you and the captain." Goatleg's face was shiny with sweat, but his eyes remained ice-hard and calm.

"You've no place to go, man. The engineer will be shutting down the boilers at any minute, and you can't keep holding all of us at bay."

"I don't intend to. Back away, both of you."

The captain said, "You damned Copperhead—"

"Back away and give me room!"

O'Hara had no doubt that Goatleg would shoot him if he failed to obey. He retreated half a dozen steps, the captain following suit.

"Very good," the fat man said. He came away from the rail and sidestepped diagonally across the deck toward that part of the taffrail which had been blown asunder by the explosion. His head swung slowly from side to side in an effort to keep everyone within the range of his vision. The derringer was steady in his hand.

"By Glory," O'Hara said, "d'you think you can go into the river and swim away?"

"That is exactly what I plan to attempt."

"You'll never make it to shore."

"Perhaps not. But then, I don't seem to have another alternative, do I?" Goatleg stopped against the splintered wood of the rail, one step from the jagged, powder-blackened hole in the deck. "I happen to be an excellent swimmer, despite my bulk, and I also happen to have a knife in my boot. I suggest no one be foolish enough to come after me." He gestured loosely with his free hand in the direction of the gambler. "Are you joining me, Colfax?"

Colfax looked frightened and unwilling to do any more gambling; he was holding a losing hand and he knew it. He stood still, shaking his head.

While this was going on, O'Hara noticed bright color out of the corner of his eye and realized for the first time that he was now standing next to the miner and the parrot. He glanced at the bird, which was glaring in a bored way in the opposite direction from all the drama. Then he looked back to Goatleg and slowly raised his left arm until the hand was at shoulder height.

The fat man said to Colfax, "Well enough, then: stay and hang. You were never really much good to the Cause—"

O'Hara grabbed the parrot by the tailfeathers and heaved upward: it flew into the air, flapping its wings wildly, squawked in surprise and outrage, said, "It's the Goddamned heathen Chinee," and then contrarily commenced a furious tirade in that same Oriental language.

The sudden williwaw drew and held Goatleg's attention for an instant, which was long enough for O'Hara to make the calculated quick draw of his own weapon.

It was also long enough for an earthenware jug to come hurtling out of the group of Mulrooney Guards on a line straight and true toward the fat man.

Goatleg saw the jug in midflight and endeavored, too late, to dodge aside. It struck him on the upper right side of the chest and threw him off-balance against the rail, then dropped at his feet wihout shattering. He retained his grip on the derringer, recovered his equilibrium, and started to raise the gun again.

O'Hara, who had been relieved by the hurled jug of the need for a hurried and therefore risky shot, fired once with careful aim.

That one shot was all that was necessary. The

bullet hit Goatleg's right wrist, jerked it up and out; the derringer flew from his grasp and plunged in an arc into the river. The fat man staggered, caught himself, and then spun and tried to leap from the deck.

One of the Mulrooneys caught hold of his coat and pulled him back. The other Guards, shouting and cursing, immediately converged on him.

There was a brief flurry of arms and legs and bodies. Just as O'Hara and the captain were about to push into them, the Mulrooneys stepped back to form a loose circle. In the middle of it Goatleg lay on his back on the sooty deck, unconscious and likely to remain so for a good while.

A roar went up from most of the passengers (those few of them, and the crew, who were Secesh sympathizers had already vacated the immediate area, since it was clearly not a good place for anyone but a Unionist). The captain, red-faced, shouted to the deckhands to put Goatleg and Bradley and Colfax into ropes, after which, without much success, he ordered everyone to clear the deck. O'Hara felt a tug on his arm and turned to be embraced by Hattie.

"Fergus, you took a terrible chance," she said. "You might have been killed."

He answered reasonably, "Aye, my lady, but I wasn't."

Billy Culligan had picked up the earthenware jug and was examining it for cracks. It appeared to have none. He withdrew the cork, wiped the powder residue from his lips, tilted the jug, and had a long draught. O'Hara disengaged himself from Hattie and went to where the Mulrooney stood.

"Billy, were you the one to throw that jug?"

"I was," Culligan said proudly. "And a fair fine toss it was, if I do say it myself. Square on the money."

"It wasn't just luck the jug hit Goatleg as it did?"

"Luck?" Culligan said. He gave O'Hara one of his reproachful looks. "Lad, there's no finer baseball pitcher on the Mulrooney team than Billy Culligan. I can be flinging the eye out of a gnat with a ball at sixty paces; hitting a man with a jug of poteen at thirty paces ain't hardly even a challenge."

O'Hara found himself grinning.

Culligan grinned back. "You did some nice work yourself, boyo," he said, and extended the jug. "Have a drap of the crature."

"I don't mind if I do," O'Hara said.

Hattie, sighing, looked on without speaking as he took the jug and drank.

⊷21⊷

Some two hours later, following the docking of the
Freebooty at the foot of Stockton's Center Street and
a goodly amount of additional activity, O'Hara stood
with Hattie and a group of men to one side of the
landing. He wore his last clean suit, a broadcloth, and
a bright green string tie in honor of St. Patrick's Day.
The others, half-circled around him, were Woodman,
the captain, the newspaperman, a hawkish man who
was Stockton's sheriff, two officials of the California
Merchants Bank, and a goateed United States Revenue officer stationed in the Stockton area. Bradley,
Goatleg and Colfax had been removed to the local jail
in the company of a pair of deputies and a doctor, and
all but a few scattered ounces of the gold was now in
the hands of the bank's representatives. The Mulrooney Guards, after minor doctoring and after prom-
ising to pay for all damages to the packet, had been
released with a reprimand.

The captain was saying, "We are all deeply in-
debted to you, O'Hara. It would have been a black
day, indeed, if you hadn't revealed those scoundrels

for what they are, and made possible the recovery of the gold.''

''I only did my duty,'' O'Hara said solemnly.

''It is unfortunate that the California Merchants Bank cannot offer you a reward, sir,'' one of the bank officials said. ''However, we are a young concern and not a wealthy one, as our urgent need of the consignment of dust can well attest. But I don't suppose you could accept a reward in any case; the Pinkertons never do, I'm told.''

''Aye, that's true.''

The Revenue agent said, ''Will you tell us now how you discovered the truth behind this entire business?''

''I will,'' O'Hara said, ''if you gentlemen will not be making my profession public hereabouts. A Pinkerton operative can ill afford to be placed in the public eye, and I have my confidential assignment to consider as well.''

He was assured that not a word would be uttered to anyone. The newspaperman said, ''Perhaps I might write a piece about the adventure for the Virginia City *Enterprise* later on; but, if so, I promise not to use your name or your profession.''

O'Hara nodded. ''Well, then, the long and the short of it, beginning with the theft of the gold,'' he said, and went on to explain about finding the bronze coin under the pilothouse sofa; his suspicions of Colfax; the reasons why he had changed his mind about the gambler at first, despite the circumstantial evidence which pointed to him. ''In the Saloon, Colfax mentioned that the war-issue cents which he considered lucky pieces are now being used in California to decorate leather goods. I pondered the possibility that the robber had been wearing such a leather article and had lost a coin from it during the theft. It turned out just so, but at the time I hadn't any direction to be pursuing it.''

Next, he explained about the clues which he had become more and more certain were in his possession. Then he looked at the newspaperman and said, "I couldn't pry loose a one of 'em—not until this morning, when you came along and gave me the one key I needed to be opening up my memory.''

The reporter was surprised. "*I* gave you the key?''

"You did," O'Hara told him. "You said of the river: 'Clear as a mirror, isn't it? It reminds me of the Mississippi when I was a boy, and of how we used to swim bare on mornings such as this. Even the strapping we would sometimes get for doing it was worthwhile.' ''

"Yes, I remember. I'm given to boyhood reminiscences on occasion. But how could that possibly have acted as a memory key?''

"Only two of the words, it was: *mirror* and *strapping*.''

Puzzled expressions.

O'Hara said, "These commenced turning over in my mind and began associating themselves with others, you see. Mirror caused me to think of reflection, and all at once I was recalling how I had been able to see a little of my own image in the pilothouse windshield not long after the robbery. Strapping caused me to think of belt, belt of leather, and leather once again of Colfax's remark concerning the coins as decoration. Next I was remembering how Bradley had his frock coat buttoned up on a warm night like the last, and how his trousers looked baggy, as though they might soon fall down—as though he weren't wearing a belt.

"Now, first off, Bradley claimed he was sitting in the pilot's seat when he heard the door open just before being struck, and that he didn't turn about because he thought it was you and the captain returning from supper. But if I was able to see *my* reflection in the glass, Bradley would sure have been able to see his—and anybody coming up behind him as well."

There were murmurs of understanding now.

O'Hara continued, "After Bradley broke open the safe and the valise and the strongbox, his problem was what to be doing with the gold. He couldn't risk a trip to his quarters while he was alone in the pilothouse; there was the possibility he might be seen, and there was also the possibility that the *Freebooty* would run into a bar or a snag if she slipped a mite off course. D'you recall saying it was a miracle such hadn't happened, Captain, thinking as you were then that Bradley had been unconscious for some minutes?"

The captain said he did.

"So, then," O'Hara said, "Bradley had to have the gold on his person when you and Woodman found him, and while I was there in the pilothouse soon afterward. He couldn't have removed it until later, when he claimed to be feeling dizzy and you helped him to his cabin. That, now, is the significance of his belt.

"What I expect he did was to take off the belt, a fine wide one decorated with war-issue cent pieces, and then with it strap the gold pouches above his

— 195 —

waist—a makeshift money belt, as it were. He was in such a rush, for fear of being discovered, that he failed to be noticing when one of the coins popped loose and rolled under the sofa.

"Once Bradley had the pouches secured, he waited until he heard Mr. Woodman and the captain returning, tending to his piloting duties all the while; then he lay down on the floor and pretended to have been knocked senseless. He kept his loose coat buttoned for fear someone would notice the thickness about his upper middle, and that he was no longer wearing his belt in his trouser loops; and he kept hitching up his trousers because he *wasn't* wearing the belt in its proper place."

Woodman said, "Well, I'm damned," and there were similar exclamations from the others.

Hattie took O'Hara's arm. "Fergus, what did Bradley do with the gold after he had removed it from the pilothouse? Did he have it all along inside his quarters, where you eventually found it?" She was well aware, of course, that he had searched Bradley's cabin the night before, along with all the others, and that the gold had not been there at that time. Nor had the coin-decorated belt.

"No, my lady," he said. "I expect Bradley was afraid of a search, so first chance he had he transferred the gold from his person to the calfskin grip. Then he hung the grip, using his belt as a cord, from a metal hook inside the gallows frame not far from his cabin."

The captain: *"Inside* the gallows frame? You mean he took the time to fasten a hook there, chancing discovery at any second?"

"It's my guess that the hook has been there for

some time, and that this isn't the first occasion young Bradley used it for purposes of his own. It wouldn't have required any time at all, then, for him to step over to the frame, slip the belt holding the grip over the hook, then return to his quarters.''

Woodman: ''How could you possibly have deduced that this was where Bradley hid the gold?''

''Another of those elusive clues,'' O'Hara said. ''While in the pilothouse after the robbery I noticed that Bradley's coat had gotten a mite gritty from his lying on the dust and soot of the floor. When I spoke to him in his cabin a while later he had changed the coat for another, and the first was draped across the back of a chair; but it was then grease-stained as well. Such grease couldn't have come from the pilothouse floor, so when the other pieces fell into place this morning, I reasoned he had to've gotten it while hiding the gold. My consideration then was that he'd have wanted a place close to his quarters, and the only such place that would have grease about it was the gallows frame.''

Hattie: ''How did you know Bradley was the one who murdered the bank employee, Stuart, in San Francisco? It might just as easily have been Goatleg or someone else.''

''Yet another clue,'' O'Hara said. He paused to light his pipe; then, once he had it drawing, he resumed. ''You see, Hattie, Stuart himself told me the name of his assassin.''

''*Stuart* told you?''

''He did. He spoke three words before he died, and at the time I thought only that they referred to the severity of his wounds. What he seemed to be saying was: 'Hurts . . . badly shot . . .' But what he was actually saying, I came to realize—his voice was too low for me to be making out the words clearly—was: 'Hurts . . . *Bradley* shot . . .' If he hadn't expired at that moment, I warrant he would have gone on to say the word *me*. 'Bradley shot me.' "

The agent (impressed): "You apparently knew Goatleg was involved in the murder of Thomas Stuart—but how?"

"A remark he made at supper last night," O'Hara told him. "He mentioned having read in the papers about the shooting of a young man near the Barbary Coast. But there was not a word in any of them of *how* Stuart had died; and I didn't tell Goatleg that it was by a bullet. The only reasonable way he could have known was either to have been the assassin himself, or to have spoken to the assassin at some later time. Once I knew Bradley was the murderer of Stuart, I also knew he and Goatleg were conjoined in that deed and so in those which took place on the *Freebooty*."

The captain: "But you also seemed to know that Goatleg was the man behind everything. Couldn't it have been another member of the Knights, such as Colfax?"

"It could have," O'Hara admitted. "But with Goatleg's apparent leadership qualities, station, and wealth, he seemed the much more likely choice."

The Revenue agent: "How did you learn that Tanner was an undercover officer for the government?"

"Only from his billfold, which I found in Bradley's cabin. I had but an inkling of it before that. Perhaps you could elaborate a bit on his task."

The agent nodded. "We have suspected for some time that Goatleg was a recruiter of funds for the Knights of the Golden Circle, as well as for the Confederate coffers in Richmond—primarily by soliciting Southern sympathizers but also through such felonious means as robbery and extortion. It was decided not to arrest him, because we had little enough evidence against him, and because we wanted the names of his cohorts and knowledge of the Golden Circle's inner workings. It was determined that infiltration of the group was the best way to accomplish our objectives, and so Tanner was brought in from the East."

Hattie: "Why did Tanner wear that fake eyepatch?"

"It was part of his pose as a Secesh," the agent said. "He claimed to Goatleg and other members of the Knights that he had lost an eye to the saber of a drunken Union cavalryman in Kansas last year, and wanted vengeance against the whole of the Union for that and other wrongs."

The Stockton sheriff: "Tanner was murdered because Goatleg and Bradley found out who he was?"

O'Hara dipped his head affirmatively. "I'll be giving you my idea of what happened, but you'll have to get the full details from either Goatleg or Bradley." He told of his confrontation with Tanner after leaving Colfax and the other players at the poker game in the Saloon. "Tanner evidently had gotten wind that the Knights intended some sort of activity on the *Freebooty,* though not precisely what it would be. So when I came questioning Colfax, he guessed that trouble was afoot and that Colfax and Goatleg were involved.

"My assumption is that he went directly to Goatleg's stateroom and perhaps overheard the blackguard conversing with Bradley. He confronted them—I expect he thought it was time to unmask himself, that he had learned enough of what he had come to learn—but was somehow overpowered and then murdered with Bradley's knife." Fergus went on to explain how he had concluded that the body had been moved from the original site of the murder back to Tanner's stateroom, and why.

He did not go on to explain, because of Hattie's presence, that Goatleg had sent Bradley after *him* with that very same knife—doubtless because the fat man had decided he was a dangerous enough adversary to justify elimination. There had not been a second attempt on his life, O'Hara postulated, because Goatleg had known he would be on guard against just such an attack, and because Bradley had botched the job once and had almost been recognized and it would have been foolish to press their luck.

Woodman: "You haven't told us, O'Hara, how you knew Goatleg and Bradley were Knights of the Golden Circle."

Fergus smiled. "It was a little bird told me so," he said.

The men looked blank, but Hattie said, "Big bird, if it's the parrot you mean."

"Aye, the parrot," O'Hara said, and then elaborated on the bird and how it had been inside Tanner's stateroom, foraging hoarhound drops, when he entered and found the body. "It spoke certain phrases then, but these sounded to me like its usual gibberish, if a mite less offensive. Hattie pointed out to me only this morning, however, the possibility that they weren't gibberish at all but a repetition of part of a conversation it had heard there in that very stateroom—a conversation, as I expect it actually happened, between Goatleg and Bradley."

"What phrases did the parrot speak?" the captain asked.

"It said: 'Men can too. Take no chances. Night sign.' "

Everyone puzzled over that for a moment. Only the Revenue agent seemed to have an inkling of what it meant; he nodded slowly and said, "Yes, of course—the Golden Circle's secret identification. We had only just learned of it; from Tanner, as a matter of fact."

Hattie: "Secret identification?"

"The Knights' sign," O'Hara said. " 'Night sign,' as the parrot spoke it."

"Ah. But what *is* the Knights' sign?"

"It has to do with a play being performed in San Francisco at present, though no one connected with it is involved with the Knights," the agent said. "A play called *Wild Horse of Tartary* in which a Miss Adah Menken has the lead role. The whole identification is rather complicated, but the sign itself is a playbill advertising the play; all Knights in the San Francisco area, and visiting from other areas, are required to carry one. There is also a ritual question-and-answer business which members of the organization who do not know each other must go through."

Hattie: "Menken. Men can too. Menken too?"

"Aye," O'Hara said. "Once Tanner's body had been returned to his stateroom, it would seem likely that Goatleg instructed Bradley to search it and Tanner's belongings, and in so instructing him spoke along such lines as: 'Take the Menken too,' referring perhaps to the playbill which Tanner would have carried in his role as a Knight. 'We must take no chances of anyone finding it and divining that it is the Knights' sign.' The parrot picked up and later spoke these phrases that I mentioned."

O'Hara asked the agent if the ritual question-and-answer business began with whether or not the individual had heard of Adah Menken; and if mention of the play, the Knights' sign, also was used between members to warn of a non-member about to enter their midst. The agent said yes to both questions. Which told O'Hara that Goatleg had probably first approached him at the Lick House because he had momentarily mistaken Fergus for a Knight—either because of his appearance or because O'Hara had just checked in and he was expecting someone. It also told him why Goatleg had mentioned the play to Colfax and Tanner in the hotel's Gentlemen's Room just prior to leaving the three of them alone together. (Tanner, however, must have still harbored suspicions with regard to O'Hara after that first meeting, which would explain why he had followed Fergus from the hotel to Portsmouth Plaza: a surveillance tactic for the purpose of learning more about him and thereby either confirming or denying O'Hara's non-affiliation with the Knights of the Golden Circle.)

He passed these explanations on to the group of men, and then relighted his pipe. "And that, now," he said, "is the sum total of it, gentlemen."

⊷22⊷

"You really are a fine detective, Fergus O'Hara," Hattie said. "That was a clever bit of deducing you did, I must say."

O'Hara said nothing. Now that they were five minutes parted from the group of men, walking alone together along Stockton's dusty main street, he had begun scowling again almost as darkly as he had during the dawn hours.

Hattie ventured brightly, "It's a splendid, sunny St. Patrick's Day, and I imagine the Mulrooney Guards are already congregating in Green Park. Shall we register at our hotel and then join the festivities, as you promised Mr. Billy Culligan?"

"We've nothing to be celebrating," O'Hara muttered.

"You're still thinking about the gold, aren't you?"

"And what else would I be thinking about?" he

said. "Fine detective—fah! Some consolation *that* is."

Hattie was silent this time.

O'Hara wondered sourly what those lads back there would say if they knew the truth of the matter: that he was no more a Pinkerton operative than the miner's parrot; that he had only been *impersonating* one toward his own ends ever since he had taken the railroad pass and letter of introduction off the chap in Saint Louis the previous year, the Pinkerton chap who'd thought he was bringing O'Hara to jail.

That he had wanted to find the murderer of Stuart and Tanner only because he intended to take the gold for himself—his own blasted freebooty.

That Fergus O'Hara was the finest damned confidence man in these sovereign United States, and the real reason he and Hattie had come to Stockton was to have for a ride a banker who expected to cheat the government by buying up Indian land.

Well, those lads never would know any of this, because he had successfully duped them all—perfectly, as always. And for nothing.

He moaned aloud, "Forty thousand in gold, Hattie. Forty thousand that I was holding right in my hands, clutched fair to my black heart, when that rascal Bradley burst in on me. Two more minutes, just two more minutes . . ."

"It was Providence," she said. "You were never meant to have that gold, Fergus."

"What d'you mean? The field was white for the sickle, as that newspaper lad put it—"

"Not a bit of that," Hattie said. "And if you'll be

truthful, you enjoyed every minute of your playacting of a detective; every minute of the explaining just now of your brilliant deductions. There's no person alive who doesn't enjoy the satisfaction of solving a difficult problem and the adulation of his peers when he does so, and you're no exception.''

"I hate mysteries," O'Hara said. "I hate detectives—"

"Bosh. Now I'm glad you brought Goatleg and the others to justice, and I'm glad you weren't able to take the gold and that it went instead to its rightful owners—and you should be too, because your heart is about as black as this sunny morning. You've only stolen from dishonest men, never decent folks, in all the time I've known you. Why, if you *had* succeeded in filching the gold, you would have begun despising yourself in less than a week—not only because it belongs to decent people, but because you would have committed the crime on St. Pat's Day. If you stopped to consider it, you wouldn't commit *any* crime on St. Patrick's Day, now would you?''

O'Hara grumbled and glowered, but he was pondering these words carefully. He was remembering, too, his thoughts in Bradley's cabin, when he had held the gold in his hands—thoughts of the captain's reputation and potential loss of position, and of the urgent need of the young branch bank in Stockton. And he was not at all sure he *would* have kept the pouches of dust even if Bradley had not burst in on him. He might just have returned them to the captain. Confound it, he might well have. And although he hated to admit it even to himself, he *had,* by damn, enjoyed being a detective and finding the solution to the mystery.

Hattie was right about St. Pat's Day, too; he just would not feel decent if he committed a crime on—

Abruptly, he stopped walking. Then he scowled again and said, "You wait here, my lady. There's a little something I've to be doing before we find our hotel and then set off for Green Park."

Hattie started to ask the obvious question, but O'Hara had already put down their luggage and was threading his way through clattering wagons and carriages to where a young towheaded boy was scuffling with a mongrel puppy. He halted before the boy. "Now then, lad, how would you be liking to have a dollar for twenty minutes' good work?"

The boy's eyes grew eager. "What do I have to do, mister?"

O'Hara removed from the inside pocket of his coat an expensive gold American Horologe watch, which happened to be in his possession as the result of disappointment, a momentary lapse of good sense, and extremely nimble fingers developed when he was a wild and foolish youth in New Orleans. He extended it to the boy. "Take this down to the *Freebooty* steamboat and look about for a tall gentleman with a mustache and a fine head of bushy hair, a newspaperman. When you've found him, give him the watch and tell him Mr. Fergus O'Hara came upon it, is returning it, and wishes him a fine and prosperous St. Patrick's Day."

"Do you know his name, mister?" the boy asked. "It might help me find him quicker."

O'Hara could not seem to recall it, if he had ever

heard it in the first place. He took the watch again, opened the hunting-style case, and discovered that a name had, indeed, been etched in flowing script on the dustcover. He handed the watch back to the boy.

"Clemens, it is," O'Hara said then. "A Mr. Samuel Langhorne Clemens . . ."